FADING

MARC JOHNSON

A SINGULARITY RISING NOVEL

A SINGULARITY RISING NOVEL

FADING

MARC JOHNSON

FADING
A Singularity Rising novel
Copyright © 2023 by Marc Johnson

Contents

CHAPTER 1

*A*LL THAT MATTERS *is the lines.* To some a blank page was terrifying, but not to Noah. It was the only way to escape his prison—the only way to escape school and let his mind be free.

As Noah crafted lines on the page, he got lost in them. It didn't even matter to him what he drew. It never did. All that mattered was how it felt. Other boys his age enjoyed video games and sports. But while he enjoyed them to a certain extent, they could never replace the art of creating a picture from the depths of his mind.

"There," Noah said. *Nothing like it at all.*

He smiled at the drawing on the sheet of paper on his desk. He had tried to replicate a stray dog he had recently come across. *It's too clean.* The fur needed to be dirty, and the lines were far too straight. *And the eyes.* The eyes were too trusting. Noah's smile transformed into a frown.

A hand shot out over his shoulder and snatched his drawing. Noah's heart rose as the piece of paper was nearly torn.

"Pretty good," Jeff said. "I wish I could draw like this. Can I have this?"

Noah took a deep breath, flaring his nostrils. He remembered that Jeff was his best friend and that he shouldn't reach out and strangle him. Not that he could. Jeff, like everyone else, was way bigger than Noah. Although gangly might be a more appropriate term to describe his friend. The tattered, leather jacket Jeff wore swallowed him whole.

Noah thought the creature looked like a store-bought dog instead of the one he'd originally wanted to draw. It was nowhere near complete, but he knew that didn't matter to Jeff. It never did. Noah shrugged. "Sure."

"Cool, thanks."

A loud voice boomed in front of the classroom. An older teacher peered over his small bifocals. "Mr. Noble and Mr. Wright, is my lesson too boring for you?"

Jeff chuckled. "Well—"

"Not at all, Mr. Hill," Noah said and shook his head.

Jeff ducked his head behind Noah. "So polite," he whispered, blowing into Noah's hair.

Noah suppressed a chuckle and snorted.

Sometimes Noah wished Jeff sat beside him instead of behind him. Noah was the one getting in trouble even though it was mostly Jeff's fault. But Jeff enjoyed sitting behind Noah and using his rather large afro as a shield from Mr. Hill and, unfortunately, also as a pencil holder. Noah rather liked his hair, in the winter anyway. It kept his head warm. In the heat of summer, he always thought about cutting it, but he never did. It could do with a trim though.

Mr. Hill continued to go over the lesson plan and Noah rubbed the bridge above his nose. He was able to understand one column of multiplication but when there were two or, God forbid, more columns, like now, it made no sense to him. What was the point of it when everyone had computers in their pockets anyway?

Noah slumped back into his chair, missing geometry. Now, shapes he could understand. He saw shapes when he drew or when he focused on animals, buildings, or people. He tapped the pencil in his fingers and bit the eraser, thinking about that dog's shape now.

No. I need to focus. With the exception of geometry, Noah's grades in math weren't good enough for his parents. He had to raise his grades to get a C average, although they wanted more.

The numbers in his workbook blurred together. It was no use. He just couldn't read numbers. He gave up and flipped to the back of the workbook. In an empty spot on the already crowded picture-filled page, he began to doodle.

Instead of feeling heavy, as it did when he worked on schoolwork, the pencil got lighter as his imagination took over. Noah quieted his mind and let his hand take over. The lines blurred until it became a shape—round. *Too round.* He needed to edge it more and let the picture come into view.

Riiing!

The school bell jolted him back to reality. He sighed at his scribbles. He hated leaving a drawing unfinished.

Jeff peered over Noah's shoulder. "I rarely see an unfinished work from you. You're lucky, Mr. Hill allows you to draw."

"It's not that," Noah said. "He's just old. Bad eyes."

Jeff shook his head. "It's more than that. Remember when Billy took out his parent's old phone and he spotted it? Or when Tricia was passing notes with her friends? Mr. Hill likes you. If he didn't, you would have been busted for drawing."

Noah zipped up his backpack and watched the aging teacher limp out of the classroom. Mr. Hill had never showed any signs of affection to Noah or anyone else before. The kids called him Mr. Over the Hill and wished he would retire already. He wasn't friendly and he didn't like to use any newer technology if he didn't have to. Because he had been there so long, the school let Mr. Hill get away with using a VCR. While Mr. Hill got on Noah about his grades, he never bothered Noah when he drew. Because of that, Noah was OK with Mr. Hill.

"Come on," Jeff said, clapping his friend on the back. "We better hurry before they start dodgeball."

"Uh, I'll be right there. I have to go to the bathroom first."

Jeff eyed him. His best friend knew Noah would sometimes skip playing and draw.

"Don't worry, I'll be there," Noah said.

"You better be," Jeff said. "If you're not out in five minutes, I'm dragging you out. And this time I mean it."

Noah put a hand up. "All right, all right."

He waited until Jeff left the classroom before grabbing his sketchbook and heading in the other direction. The kids flooded the hallway and Noah squeezed by them. He wished he were bigger so he could push instead of being pushed. He had to finish that drawing. It was like an itch in the back of his mind. He would hide out in the bathroom like he sometimes did. Noah knew Jeff wouldn't come. He never did. Maybe it was because Jeff knew how Noah was, or maybe it was because Jeff got too absorbed in the game, much as Noah did with his drawings. Noah would have to make it up to him. As much as he hated it, tomorrow he would play dodgeball with his friend.

When he got to the bathroom, he peeked inside. No one was there. He hurried into one of the stalls, knowing that he didn't have much time.

When the school bell finally rang, that itch in the back of his head subsided. He let out a sigh of relief. The drawing wasn't the best—he hadn't had enough time—but he would finish it at home or, more likely, during the rest of Mr. Hill's class. Noah exited the stall and ran smack into a rather large kid, and one who hated his guts.

CHAPTER 2

"OOOF," NOAH SAID as his face smashed into Frank's large and smelly torso. Frank pushed him off and Noah crashed back into the closed bathroom door.

"Watch where you're going," Frank said.

Noah didn't meet his eyes. "Sorry." He didn't want to provoke Frank—not today. He tried to slink by Frank but Frank blocked his path. "Come on. I don't want to be late for class."

"Then you shouldn't have bumped into me." Frank snatched Noah's notebook.

"Hey! Give that back!" Noah tried to grab it, but Frank held it out of arm's reach. Noah clenched his fists. Frank was so much bigger and stronger than he was. Everyone was bigger than he was. His dad said that he would grow taller and fill out in a few years, much like he had. It didn't feel that way to Noah. If it weren't for his puffy afro, he'd feel smaller than he already was. And if it weren't for his hair, he wouldn't be noticed at all.

Frank bent down, dangling Noah's notebook in front of him. "Here, kitty, kitty, kitty."

Noah's shoulders slumped. He sighed, trying to look defeated, before leaping up for the notebook. It slipped through his fingertips as Frank pulled it away.

"Oooh, nice try," Frank said with a wicked grin on his face. "What's this?" Frank had flung the notebook open and the drawings drew Frank's attention. "This page is my favorite. Mind if I keep it?"

Before Noah could say anything Frank ripped the page from the book. He didn't rip it from its spine. Frank tore the drawing in half. Noah's mouth was agape as he watched. No matter how angry Noah was, he knew there was nothing he could do about it.

It was as if Frank had torn into his soul. Noah had never destroyed any of his drawings. Sure, he had given them away, but he never ripped them or trashed them.

Much to his parents' chagrin, the overflowing boxes, and the walls of his room, attested to the fact that he kept every single one of them.

Staring at Noah's face, Frank's eyes widened and he grinned. "Let me see what other drawings I like."

"No!" Noah said, frantically reaching out in vain as Frank shoved him away.

Frank dangled it in front of Noah as if he were a cat, but this wasn't a string. It was his life's work.

"Boys," a piercing voice said. "You heard the bell. You're late for class."

Behind Frank stood a tall, slim woman, her bright, blond hair tied up into a bun. Her sharp, dark blue eyes stared at them. "Francis, give Noah back his notebook and get to class."

"Yes, Ms. Vera," Frank said, lowering his head. He tossed the notebook at Noah before skulking down the hallway.

It struck Noah in the face but he didn't care. He bent down, retrieving the torn page that Frank had so kindly stepped on as he walked away. Noah did his best to flatten it out. If he took a pencil and darkened in the lines, maybe he could use the smudges from Frank's shoes as hair, or perhaps—

"Noah," Ms. Vera said, her voice softening. "If you'd please come with me."

He nodded, grabbing his backpack.

"Have you done any more drawings lately?" she asked.

"Uh-huh. Would you like one?"

She smiled at him. "I would love one."

Even though he drew a lot, Noah rarely gave away his drawings. He only gave them to people he cared about and was close to. Ms. Vera had saved Noah from...Francis. Noah barely contained a chuckle. None of the other kids ever called Frank by his real name. Those that did got a beating for their bravery or stupidity.

Ms. Vera had been Noah's 3rd grade teacher last year. He missed her. She was a better and friendlier teacher than Mr. Hill even if she hadn't let him draw as much as he did.

"You know, Noah, I had plenty of experiences with bullies when I was your age."

"Uh-huh." He rolled his eyes. As much as he liked her, she was going to give him the same speech adults always gave kids when it came to bullying. They always said that you should ignore them and that things will be different when you're older.

"You should never back down from bullies," she said. "If you give an inch, they'll take a mile." She stopped and faced Noah. "And the older you get, the worse it gets. Understand?"

It does. He nodded. It was so rare that adults told the truth, and he appreciated it when they did.

Ms. Vera smiled. "Good." She continued walking and he hurried to keep pace with her. "I'm glad I ran into you, Noah," Ms. Vera said. "I need you to do something for me."

"What is it, Ms. Vera?"

She stopped in front of her classroom, and there stood a girl Noah had never seen before.

She's tall.

The girl had long black hair, partially covering her face. Her green eyes looked large behind the big spectacles she wore. It reminded him of an anime Jeff had showed him once.

"Noah," Ms. Vera said. "I want you to meet our newest student, Mikayla."

"Please, Ms. Vera, Mika," the girl said, "It's much easier to say. My mom thought 'Mikayla' would sound respectful, but I've never liked it."

"I like it," Noah said, smiling. "It's unique." The heat in his cheeks rose and he turned away.

"See?" Ms. Vera said. "Noah likes it. Noah, Mika is going to be in your class. Mr. Hill already knows she's coming. What I need you to do is show her around and help her out around school. Can you do that?"

He nodded. "Yes."

"Good. Now get to class. You're already late. Mika, if you need anything please come see me. Noah, I want you to take good care of her."

"I will."

They walked back to class. *The first thing I should teach her about is our teacher.* "Mr. Hill isn't like Ms. Vera. He's..."

"A grumpy old man. That I'm used to. A lot of teachers are like that these days. Ms. Vera seems nice. Shame I'm not in her class."

"You would like her. I did. I had her last year, but I've known her ever since I've been here. I wish she taught older kids but she doesn't. Here we are." He opened the door for her.

"Mr. Noble," Mr. Hill said, peering over his glasses. "You're late."

"Sorry, but Ms. Vera wanted me to bring the new student to class."

Mr. Hill grunted. He took Mika's transfer papers without so much as a "hi." "These look to be in order. Class, this is Mikayla."

"Mika," she said.

"Hmmm, right. Please, Ms. Niama, find an empty seat."

Noah watched her as she scanned the classroom. In a room of nearly thirty kids, there were three empty seats. There was the one in the back with the wobbly desk that no one wanted—yet the school never took it away or fixed it. The other one was near Tricia and her group of girls. He thought Mika would go there. Ever since Ally had moved away, Tricia had been looking for another girl to complete her foursome...or her gruesome as he and Jeff called them.

Tricia whispered to Lainey and Dany as she eyed Mika. Noah shook his head. He'd never understand girls. Not that he ever wanted to. He couldn't even understand his mom, and he loved her.

The last seat was next to him, but he doubted Mika would sit there. Especially since Tricia waved to Mika to sit near her and her cronies.

Noah sighed before opening his text book again. This time he would concentrate and not draw. At least until the lesson was done. Then he would draw again. He would always draw, no matter how old he got.

"Hey stranger, this seat taken?"

Noah looked up into Mika's magnified eyes and big smile. He cleared his throat. "No?"

Jeff leaned forward, whispering into Noah's afro. "Are you going to introduce me?"

Noah rolled his eyes and said, "Mika, this is my annoying friend, Jeff."

"Mr. Noble and Ms. Niama," Mr. Hill's grumpy old voice boomed from the front of the classroom. "Pay attention to the lesson plan."

"Sorry, Mr. Hill," Mika said. She smiled at Noah, suppressing a giggle.

Mr. Hill's droning voice continued the lesson and Noah like everyone else in the class, struggled to stay awake. He yawned and, for once, the school bell was on his side. As the students grabbed their lunches and headed for the door, Noah caught Mika's green eyes. *Maybe I should ask her to lunch with me and Jeff.* It would be nice to make another friend even if it was a girl.

But before he could even muster up the courage to ask her, Tricia and her cronies dragged her away. Noah gave her a weak smile, watching her leave.

"Well," Jeff said, putting his scrawny arm around his friend. "That was good while it lasted. She seemed nice. Now we've lost her forever."

"You don't know that," Noah said, staring at the empty seat beside him. Still, his friend wasn't completely wrong. That's how Lainey had ended up near

Tricia. In the second grade, Noah and Lainey had been good friends. Now their conversations weren't much more than politeness.

He resigned himself to their routine, and the pair sat at a small table by themselves. Noah gave Jeff half of his sandwich and chips. He didn't mind. He never ate much and his parents always packed more than enough for him. Noah always kept his cookie though. There were lines.

"You sure you don't want to come along?" Jeff said with a mouthful of sandwich. He rose from the table, his body poised to leave.

Noah shook his head. "I still haven't finished my lunch."

"OK, if you change your mind you know where to find me." Jeff took off, wanting to go play games with the other kids before lunch finished. That was fine by Noah. He wanted to be by himself and draw. Noah took one last glance at Mika, on the other side of the cafeteria, before getting out his pencil and an earlier drawing.

Noah stared at the five-story building, wondering how much shade he should put against the ground. Just a few more details and he would be done. Then it could go into one of his boxes under the bed. He stuck out his tongue, licking his lips, and a sharp pain dug into his back.

"Ow!" He turned around, seeing a familiar freckled face with large glasses staring back at him.

"I found you!" Mika said, grinning at him. "I came over to sit with you, but you were gone."

He frowned. "I've been right here the whole time. I like to draw during lunch. How come you're not with Tricia?"

Before Mika could answer, Tricia came over with Lainey and Alicia. "Mika, there you are," Tricia said. "I thought you were going to throw away your lunch."

"I did, and now I'm here."

"Why'd you come here?" Tricia said, twirling her hair. "We were just about to go outside."

"I came to talk to Noah."

Tricia rolled her eyes. "Oh God. Why would you ever want to do that? No one ever pays much attention to Noah."

"He's right here," Mika said, pushing up her glasses on her nose.

"I don't know," Lainey said, from behind Tricia. "I've always liked his drawings. He's pretty good."

"Ugh," Tricia said. "Whatever. Fine. He's quite forgettable and quite small. Come on, girls. Let's go."

"Bye, Lainey," Noah said as they passed by.

The girl smiled but didn't say a word.

"You didn't have to do that," Noah said, looking up at Mika. "You could have gone with them."

She shook her head as she sat down. "Nah. Girls like that I don't care for. All style and no substance. Me, I much prefer tech. Besides, I still need you to show me around just as Ms. Vera said."

"Oh." He glanced back down at his notebook. "I can show you around later. You'll be disappointed in the computer lab. We all are. Because we're only ten, they give us old equipment."

"That would be great. My mom says I need to get out more, but what's the point, when we have the Internet? We're all connected." She leaned in close. "How did you do that?"

"Do what?"

"Disappear. I was walking to you when you vanished."

He paused. "I didn't do anything. I was sitting here the whole time." He looked around the nearly empty cafeteria. "I think the other kids blocked your view, or maybe your glasses got a smudge on it or something."

Mika took off her glasses, cleaning them. Noah hadn't realized how green her eyes were, and he smiled.

"What?" she asked. "Is there something on my face?"

"No, nothing."

Mika cupped her chin. "I could have sworn you were there, then I just sort of forgot about you." She shook her head. "I don't think I was imagining things."

"You did bump into me," Noah said.

She laughed. "Sorry. My mom says I sit too close to the screen and that I'm making my eyes worse. She might be right, but don't tell her that."

Noah smiled back. "I won't." He stared back down at his notebook, the pencil twitching in his hand.

Mika gasped. "Wow. Lainey was right. You *are* good. Are you done?" Her eyes stared at him.

"I can't finish with someone staring at me." He closed the notebook. "Come on. I'll show you around the school."

Mika grinned. "It's about time."

Noah had never been a tour guide before. He had been asked to do things before, but the teachers never followed up with him once he started drawing. He enjoyed spending time with Mika, but it was weird. He had never talked so much before, not even with Jeff. She was just so inquisitive.

"Man, the computers at this school are really old," Mika said as they stood in the computer lab. Her mouth hung open. "You weren't kidding."

Noah stared up at her. "You have a thing for computers, don't ya?"

She smiled and shrugged. "Yeah, I do. I love them. It's the one thing I have with me whenever me and my mom move. And we move a lot. I'm gonna do something with computers when I grow up. Not sure what though. A computer programmer sounds pretty boring."

"How about a hacker like in the movies?"

Mika turned to him and a sly smile crossed her face. "Oh Noah, hacking is nothing like the movies at all."

"But aren't you at a computer typing like a programmer? Sounds like the same thing."

Mika cupped her chin. "You may be right. But it's far more exciting to get into somewhere you're not supposed to. And a challenge too."

Noah was thankful by the time the bell rang. He ran to the nearest fountain, slurping and gulping the lukewarm water. While his throat was sore, his lips were dry, and he hadn't even finished the drawing as he'd thought he would, he'd had such a good time with Mika.

As soon as Noah sat down, Jeff leaned in and whispered, "Did you have fun? I didn't realize you were going to show her around school. I would have went."

"You can go next time," Noah said.

Jeff blew a lock of his hair, dangling in front of his forehead. "Sure."

Mr. Hill's droning voice began and Noah slumped in his seat. He straightened up, stifling a yawn. *Focus.* But it was hard. His belly was full and he was tired from showing Mika around. She had long legs and he didn't. There was also the drawing he hadn't finished. *The background needs work.*

Noah sighed. *As soon as I finish this then I'll concentrate on Mr. Hill's lesson plan.* At least that's what he always told himself. He much preferred teachers like Ms. Vera. She understood a kid's mind tended to wander, and she was far more creative than teachers like Mr. Hill.

As his mind sharpened and focused on his drawing, the pressure in his mind eased.

"Ow!" Noah yelled as sharp fingernails dug into his skin.He pulled his arm away, seeing Mika staring at him.

"Mr. Noble!" Mr. Hill said. "Is there a reason you're interrupting my class?"

Noah glared at Mika and shook his head. "Sorry, Mr. Hill. An annoying bug bit me. It won't happen again."

He leaned to the side and said to Mika, "What'd you do that for?"

"Did you not see that? You vanished!" Her large eyes nearly bulged from her head.

"Shhh!" Noah said. "I did not! And stop saying that!"

"What are you two babbling about?" Jeff asked.

"You didn't see it either?" Mika said. She stared into Noah's eyes, and in a calm voice that chilled his soul, she said, "I swear to God, you were gone."

CHAPTER 3

GONE? *What did she mean gone?*

The question lingered in Noah's mind, and he wasn't able to draw for the rest of the day, which would have taken his mind off it. On top of that, Mika wouldn't stop staring at him or pestering him about it. He stared at his hands for the rest of the day, trying to catch a glimpse of whether she had spoken of was true. But neither he nor Jeff, who had sat behind him, had noticed anything like that. With all the students in the class, if Mika were right, someone would have seen it by now. She must have been mistaken.

The final bell rang, and Noah grabbed his backpack and jetted out of the room. He didn't even say good-bye to Jeff. Usually, being so small was a hindrance, but because of it, he was able to slip between all the other students, making his way down the hall. Mika was calling his name.

Noah paused, seeing his nemesis, Frank, about fifteen feet in front of him. He didn't have time to be stopped by that large mound. Not today. Neither Mika nor Frank would catch him.

Noah spun around, slipping between two sixth graders and out through the side entrance. He glanced back, relieved Mika wasn't behind him. He sighed, seeing the long staircase ahead of him. There was a reason Noah didn't come this way. *So many stairs,* and he was ill-equipped to climb them.

He started the long climb up, his backpack becoming heavier with each step. Several times he moved to the side to let the older, bigger kids go by. How he envied their size and strength. He gasped for air several times, hating how the sweat dripped down his armpits and coated his body. His clothes stuck to him, and he pulled the grimy clothes away from his skin.

"Need some help?"

Noah lifted his tired head, wiping the sweat from his brow. A familiar face sported a rather large smile.

He didn't say anything. Not because he didn't want to, but because he couldn't.

"You're a tough find," she said. She dug into her bag and pulled out a reusable water bottle. "Here."

"Thanks," Noah said, gulping it down. He handed it back to her. "You know, I would have been farther away if it wasn't for all these stairs. Next to math, I hate stairs."

"I'm glad you're going in my direction."

"Really? I thought your parents would have picked you up on your first day of school."

Mika shrugged. "My mom doesn't have time. She barely had enough time to drop me off, and I was late. Single mom and all. I have to get to know the area anyway. Going to have to get here on my own tomorrow morning. You can show me around, and we can talk about your disappearing act." She hooked her arm into his.

Noah groaned. "Can't wait."

During their walk, Mika kept bugging Noah about his disappearance. She never accepted his answer that he didn't know anything, so he kept deflecting her questions.

Noah pointed. "See that old house on the corner? Stay away from it. There's a crazy cat lady there and it stinks."

"Uh-huh."

"And that house with the wooden fence, there's a hole in it and you can squeeze through it and cut through the yard. Mr. and Mrs. Sandeep don't seem to mind. It'll take you to the other street if you're in a hurry or trying to run away from a stray dog or something."

But no matter how much he tried to distract her, she was focused on his disappearing. When they finally got to where she lived, she seemed to give up, which he was thankful for.

Mika lived not too far from the school, though in the opposite direction from home. A cluster of apartment buildings was hidden between the thickets of maple trees. In the center of the complex was a wide-open space with freshly cut grass and paved walkways leading from the apartments to the parking lots and dumpsters.

Mika and her mother lived at the top of an apartment building. *Great. More stairs.* Mika plopped her backpack on the floor and threw her jacket on the couch. Half-opened boxes filled the small apartment and dishes were stacked on the floor, along with folded blankets, rolled-up towels, and piles of books. Mika navigated the unpacked stuff with ease. Noah tiptoed around them, but he knocked over a glass. It clanked on the carpet floor but didn't break.

"Whew," he said.

"Don't worry about it." Mika never looked over and, in the corner of the apartment, she booted up her laptop.

Noah took off his shoes.

"What are you doing?" Mika asked.

"Taking off my shoes."

She waved her hand. "Keep them on. We've got more important things to do. We need to figure out how you're able to do that disappearing act."

Noah ran his fingers through his matted afro. "I'm telling you, I can't disappear. You were seeing things." He peered forward. "When was the last time you had your eyes checked?"

Mika stuck her chest out. "Rude!"

"Well?"

She exhaled. "Fine. A few months ago, at my last school."

"You sure you don't need to finish unpacking?" he said, glancing around the small apartment.

"Me and my mom never stay in any one place long. This might be as good as it gets."

Noah sighed. Clearly she wasn't going to stop with this. "All right, if I try to disappear again, will you let me go home? I can't stay out too late. My parents will worry."

"Of course. I'm not a monster. If you do disappear, you can always stay for dinner. Do you like ramen or mac and cheese out of a box?"

Noah made a face. His parents always cooked him a meal. Although he did enjoy the occasional fast food they had. "No thanks. I'll pass."

"Good," she said, clapping her hands. "I'm too excited to eat anyway." Mika licked her lips, staring at Noah as neither of them said a word.

"OK, but can you not stare at me?"

"Sure."

Noah sat down cross-legged on the floor and closed his eyes. Mika didn't say a word, but he could feel her intense stare. He opened his eyes, looking at her.

"Sorry, sorry," Mika said. She moved away from him, settling in on the other side of the living room.

"This is ridiculous," Noah mumbled under his breath. As nice as Mika was, this whole disappearing act was crazy. He'd make it a point to stay away from her from now on. *That's what I get for helping out the New Girl.* But as soon as he tried and failed, he could go home, to a nice home-cooked meal and to drawing. And probably his homework, as his parents would want him to get it done.

Noah closed his eyes for nearly a full minute. He didn't feel any different and Mika didn't make a sound. He opened his eyes. "There, are you happy now? Can I go?"

She squinted. "Are you sure you tried?"

"Yes. I need to go. It's getting late."

"But you just got here," Mika said. "Wait! I have an idea." She ran into the bedroom, and came back with a clipboard, a piece of paper, and a pencil. Here, sit at the table."

"What do you want me to do? I need to go."

"Come on, *please.*"She seemed on the verge of tears, and Noah allowed himself to be pulled to the table.

"Fine," he said. "What do you want me to do?"

"Draw me a picture, please. Something I can hang on the fridge and show my mom."

"OK." Noah stared at the blank sheet of paper and bit his lower lip. This he could do. Not vanish, but draw.

Noah forgot about the strange new girl, the fact that he had just met her and was in her apartment, and the homework and chores he needed to do later. All he concentrated on was the blank page, and he let his imagination run wild.

The tension in his head cleared when he drew, as it always did. He let out a sigh. Drawing was as satisfying as getting a scoop of ice cream on a hot summer's day or finding a dollar bill in one of his parents' pants when he did the laundry.

He had no idea what to draw, but then he remembered Mika's large green eyes. They reminded him of something, and his fingers moved without thought.

"There," Noah said when he finished. He smiled at the chameleon. He still needed to enlarge the branch it stood on and add some leaves. Not to mention drawing more lines in the skin.

"Oh. My. God." Mika squealed. Noah had forgotten she was there, but he couldn't forget now, as she had a phone in his face. "You're not going to believe this," she said.

Mika sat down next to him, showing him the video. It was weird seeing himself on camera. He squirmed, not liking it, and he heard his mom's voice telling him to sit up straight and smile for the camera.

He gasped when he saw it. His body was faded away. The camera was still on him, but there was nothing there. Where he should have been, he wasn't. Even the pencil he held and the paper he touched couldn't be seen. Yet he didn't remember disappearing. There had been no strange sensation and no sparkling light like he had seen in movies.

He stopped and turned to Mika. Her eyes were still fixated on the phone. "Did you use some kind of new filter? Is this a trick?"

"Uh-uh. This is no trick." Mika set the phone down, and her eyes turned toward him. "You vanished! I was staring at you and then you faded from my sight. I even forgot you were there until you stopped drawing." She didn't blink. "How did you do that?"

"I'm-I'm not sure." Noah shook his head. He grasped his chest, having a hard time breathing. *Was that real?*

"Did you feel any different?"

"No...no. I—I'm sorry, I need to go." Noah rushed from his seat, grabbed his backpack, and headed toward the door.

"Wait!" Mika said.

He hesitated, afraid that another camera might be in his face or that she thought he was a freak.

Instead, Mika gave him the sweetest smile and glanced down at the drawing on the table. "Thanks for coming over and thanks for the drawing. I love it."

Noah blushed before slipping out the door. In a hushed tone he said, "You're welcome."

As he made his way home, he leaned against the buildings in Mika's complex, then on the wooden fences that surrounded some of the houses on the block. He wiped the sweat from his brow and breathed in, wondering why he was so tired.

He glanced at his hands. *Disappearing takes a lot more out of me than I thought.* But he couldn't worry about that now. All he thought about was that video Mika had recorded. A video he didn't even tell her to destroy or not show anyone.

Idiot.

What would his parents think, or Jeff, if they knew he could vanish like that? Frank was right. He was a freak. On the way home, Noah tried to make himself disappear, but he looked at every car window he passed and he was still there.

What does it all mean?

Noah reached his home far more quickly than he'd thought he would. As much as he ached to draw, he thought that walking home would help him clear his mind of all his crazy thoughts. But he never got the chance.

The house his parents had bought when he was born was larger than it had any right to be, with four bedrooms and two bathrooms. They had moved away from the big city because prices were cheaper and they wanted to start a big family. After all these years, they only had Noah. He wanted a little brother or sister, but as the years passed, he'd given up on that.

Noah burst through the front door, wanting to get upstairs before his mom saw him.

"Noah!" she yelled.

Too late. He poked his head in the kitchen. Being Asian, his mom was shorter than most women her age. Yet it was that same blood that kept her from aging. Aside from the hair, Noah took after his mom more than his dad. Unfortunately, his height came from his mom. It would be nice to be taller.

Mom was busy cooking dinner. The sizzling sounds from the pan rang in his ears, and the smell of seared chicken floated through his nose. He hoped his mom burned the edges just the way he liked it. Noah licked his lips. He was hungry. Mom stood in front of a chopping board, dicing up vegetables. Too many vegetables for his taste.

"Yes, mom?" he asked.

"Where have you been? she asked. She peered more closely at his face. "Are you OK? You look pale. Are you sick?"

"I'm fine." At least he was fine now. He was no longer winded, but he was a little tired. He yawned. "It's just been a long day."

"Uh-huh." She glanced at his feet. "Shoes. Where were you and why were you so late?"

"Sorry," Noah said, taking off his shoes. "I was at a friend's house."

"Jeff's?"

"No." He hesitated. "Someone else."

"Oh. Who?"

He'd been hoping she wouldn't ask this, as he had a feeling he might regret it. "Some new girl from school."

She put down the spatula and put a hand to her hip. A sly smile spread on her face. "Who's the girl?"

The heat in Noah's neck rose and he turned away. *I knew I shouldn't have told her anything.* "I don't know. Ms. Vera asked me to show her around so I did and we...hung out after school. That's all." He didn't dare tell his mom about how he could vanish in thin air.

The smile across her face got even wider. "I see. Is she pretty?"

Noah rolled his eyes. "Mom." He ducked back out of the kitchen and headed upstairs.

"Get washed up, dinner's almost ready and your father will be here soon."

"OK," he yelled back.

As soon as Noah got inside his room, he dropped his heavy backpack, closing the door and leaning against it until his butt slid down and hit the floor. He still didn't completely believe Mika's video. But what else could it have been?

In the movies, they always saw their hands disappear or the light hurt their eyes, but Noah didn't feel any different when he did it. But life was never like the movies.

What am I going to do?

CHAPTER 4

NOAH WOKE up late because of Mr. Hill's homework. Going to Mika's apartment had cost him time, and he couldn't concentrate on anything but that video. He didn't even feel like drawing. He wanted to get to school first and talk to her—tell her not to show the video to anyone. No matter how fast he ran—or waddled, with all the weight behind him—he never gained much ground.

He made it to school maybe five minutes before the first bell rang. He leaned over and panted, searching for her. *There!* Over near the tetherball courts was Mika, but she wasn't alone. She had pulled out her phone and was showing Jeff the video she'd recorded last night.

No! Noah dropped his bag and ran to them. *Oh please! Let it be a cool video or new game or stupid animal trick.* Plenty of kids took out their phones before and after school, showing exactly that. Yet when he reached them, the stunned expression on Jeff's face told him everything he needed to know.

"You told him!" Noah said, gasping for breath. "Why did you tell him? Did you tell anyone else?"

Mika shook her head. "No. Why would I?"

"I'm your best friend," Jeff said, putting a hand to his chest. "I'm not gonna tell anyone. I can't believe you weren't gonna tell me. *I* should be mad at *you.*"

It wasn't that. Noah didn't want his best friend to think he was some kind of monster. But as Noah looked into his friend's eyes, he didn't see that. Noah nodded. "You're right."

"Can you really disappear?" Jeff asked, his face getting closer as his eyes probed him.

Noah leaned back. "I don't know. Mika says I can, but it doesn't feel that way."

Mika pushed her glasses up before shoving the phone in his face. "That's not what the camera says, and I *saw* you disappear!"

"All right, all right," Noah said, covering her mouth. "Lower your voice before someone hears you. Do you know how crazy this sounds?"

Riiing!

The kids around them put their phones away before scattering and heading back inside to their respective classes. As the rest of their classmates melted away, all that was left was the trio.

"I need to see this." Jeff's finger inched closer to Noah's shoulder.

Noah slapped his hand away. "I'm not going to do it now. Come on, we need to get to class. You know how Mr. Hill gets if someone is late."

Despite how tired Noah was, he outran his friends back to class. Not that he was in any hurry to get to Mr. Hill's class, but it was the only way to escape being asked a ton of questions by the other two. Since they sat next to him, Noah knew it was going to be a long day.

It was hard to pay attention to today's lesson, and it had nothing to do with Mr. Hill. Mika and Jeff kept staring at him. In fact, Jeff kept poking him every few minutes to see if he was still there. Noah almost started drawing again, but Mika's gaze sharpened when he did so.

He was relieved when the first bell rang. He was the first one sprinting out of class, saying he had to use the restroom. He headed in the opposite direction, slipping between the rushing kids, and ended up in the hallway where the older kids' classrooms were.

Noah leaned against the lockers, panting for breath as sweat formed on his forehead. He knew he shouldn't avoid Jeff and Mika, but he just needed a second to think. They were bound to have so many questions and he didn't have any answers for them. He was still trying to get over his shock over what he could do.

The heavy footsteps thumping behind Noah froze him. His spine stiffened as he remembered what section of the school he was in and who had a class there.

"What do we have here?"

Frank.

"You know this part of the school isn't for little pipsqueaks like you," Frank said.

"I—"

Frank shoved him and he fell against the ground. Noah scrambled away, but the bigger kid stalked him, cutting off every avenue of escape.

"Frank," Noah said, taking a step back. "I don't have time for this. Don't you want to go outside? It's recess, and you know how short they are these days."

Frank grinned, rolling up his sleeves. "I'd much rather be here. And this time there's no teacher to save you."

I really shouldn't have come here.

Noah's eyes went wide as Frank approached. At times like this he wished he were bigger, stronger, or faster or could disappear.

That's it!

Noah clenched his fists and closed his eyes, willing with all his might to disappear just like Mika had said he could. He clamped down on his teeth, and he had never wished for anything so hard in his life. He knew he could do it if he just concentrated hard enough.

When he opened his eyes, Frank's meaty fist swung toward him, smacking into his face. He crashed into the locker, yelping in pain as the locker's combination dug into his back. He got up and wiped the blood from his nose.

Tears welled up in Noah's eyes. Not from the pain or the blood but at his own foolishness at thinking he could disappear at will. Then he remembered his new friend and how he disappeared in the first place.

Drawing.

There was no time to draw here, but Noah stood up and closed his eyes, tightening his shoulders for another of Frank's blows.

Frank slammed into the lockers on the other side of the hall.

"Watch it, meathead!" Mika said, appearing next to Noah. She rubbed her shoulder.

"What do you think you're doing, New Girl?" Frank said. "Don't think I won't hit a girl or someone with glasses? Equal rights and all that."

"Leave them alone," Jeff said, strolling up to his friends and rolling up his sleeves. "Now." The look on Jeff's face reminded Noah of the time that Noah crouched behind Frank's legs and Jeff slammed into him. It was the one time they had beaten Frank together.

"This has nothing to do with you," Frank said.

Noah looked at his buddy, relieved to find him here. Jeff had saved Noah from Frank many times. Jeff may not have been as large or as strong as Frank, but when he fought it was ferocious. Jeff lost against Frank more often than not, but he made sure Frank remembered him.

Frank glared at the three of them in silence. He clenched his meaty fists. "Bah! I don't want to waste any more of my recess on you three." He bullied pass them, heading down the hall.

"You OK?" Mika asked, pulling a crumbled napkin from her pocket. Her tender touch wiped the blood from Noah's face.

He sighed. "No. I'm getting tired of Frank."

"Then maybe we can do something about it," Jeff said.

"What do you mean?"

"If you can disappear, maybe it's time to turn the tables on ol' Francis there." Jeff sported a devilish grin, and Noah knew what that meant.

Jeff opened his mouth but Noah put a hand up. "After school. I don't want to hear any more about my disappearing 'till after then. OK?"

"OK."

He looked to Mika.

"OK."

"Thanks. I can't concentrate in Mr. Hill's class with you two pestering me all the time, waiting for me to disappear."

"Sounds good to me."

"Me too," Mika said.

The bell rang and the three walked back to class together.

"Meathead?" Noah asked, chuckling. "That's Frank all right."

Mika rolled her eyes. "Ugh. It's something my mom says. Seemed appropriate."

CHAPTER 5

AFTER THE INCIDENT with Frank, Noah was able to relax again. He was even almost able to draw, although Mika kept stealing glances at him. But he was afraid to. He needed a place where he could try to disappear again. A place away from prying eyes—be it teachers or his parents.

As the hours passed, Noah thought of his plan and where he would go after school. The final bell rang and Noah led Jeff and Mika away from the school building.

"You taking us to your house?" Jeff asked. He kicked a rock as they passed by. "We can use that spare bedroom your parents have. I'm sure your mom would love to meet Mika." He snickered and Noah ignored him and rolled his eyes.

"No. You remember Mr. and Mrs. Robeson, and how for two years before they died, I walked their dog, Patch, for them?"

Jeff nodded. "I remember. They were nice. I really miss them, and their homemade cookies." He licked his lips.

"I miss them too. They were such a sweet old couple and had a nice dog." Noah paused. "I never told you this, but one day, that dog chased a squirrel off this sidewalk and into the woods."

"You went into the woods?" Jeff asked. "I thought you hated nature."

Noah made a face. "I don't hate nature. I'm just not a fan of bugs and their bites."

"Me neither," Mika said, rubbing her arms. "I need a computer and a power pack and good Wi-Fi."

Jeff laughed. "You two are terrible."

Noah and Mika shared a smile.

Mika and Jeff chatted while Noah led them on their sidewalk quest. The houses in the area weren't as tightly packed as those in the city. That's why Noah's parents had moved to this area in the first place. They wanted to get away from the rush and stinky smells of the city and raise their kids in a better place.

Noah always had a hard time remembering exactly where the entrance lay, but he knew it was next to the light blue house on the corner with the broken fence. If that didn't remind him, there was the large cracked sidewalk. A tree's root had undergrown it, but the city had never gotten around to fixing it.

"Here it is," Noah said, stopping right on top of the crack.

While rows of trees lingered on the edge of the sidewalk, shading the homes, there was a cluster of three small grove trees hugging together. Their leaves covered the entrance, but the three kids squeezed through the opening between the trunks. The tall shrubs brushed against Noah's arms and legs.

"Ugh," Mika said, swatting away a fly. "How much farther?"

"Not too far." Noah ducked under a branch and said, "There."

A large tree, surrounded by large bushes, had fallen over some time ago. A faded green tent had been draped over it and staked to the ground. The tent's lines were tied around the trunk.

Noah rushed to it and secured a loose line, tightening up the tent. "Sorry I haven't been here in a few weeks. I was going to come out this weekend."

"What is this place?" Jeff asked.

Noah shrugged. "My hideout. Like I said, I found it walking Patch one day." Noah looked up. "Or Patch led me to this place."

"And this is what you did with that old tent my dad was going to throw out."

"Yeah, it seemed like a waste. I'm glad I found this place. My parents are always yammering about how I should 'get out of the house and turn off that screen.' 'Back in my day,' blah, blah, blah. Whenever they do that, I come here. It's not too bad if you don't mind all the bugs in the summer and the chill in the winter. Sorry, Mika, the signal out here is kind of spotty."

"It's OK."

Noah opened up the flap and let his two friends go inside. On the tent's floor, papers, worn out pencils, and dried-up pens were scattered about. An opened and empty box of cookies lay there along with candy wrappers and half-empty bottles of water.

Noah started to tidy up the place and make more room. "Watch your head." There was barely enough room for the three of them, and they all stood uncomfortably close to each other.

"Sorry, I'm not used to having people over. Otherwise, I would have brought more snacks and cleaned things up. But I figured we needed a quiet and private place if we're going to do this. I'm not sure how hard this is going to be and how long it's going to take, but I'm willing to give it my best shot."

Jeff clasped his hand on Noah's shoulder. "Don't worry about it. This is great." He squinted at him. "Hey, were you ever going to tell me about this place?"

Noah took a pick out and straightened his hair. "Ummm...we better hurry up before our parents wonder where we are."

"So how does this work exactly?" Jeff asked.

Noah opened his mouth, but Mika interrupted him.

"Noah's not able to access his ability when he wants to, at least not yet." She smiled at him. "Don't worry, we'll get there. But I've noticed that whenever Noah draws, he's able to tap into that power of his. I'm not sure why. Is it because he doesn't notice he's doing it, or is it because he can only do it while drawing?"

"This true?" Jeff asked Noah.

"Uh-huh. Far as I can tell."

"I hope it's not something you can only do while drawing," Jeff said. "Then it'd be useless."

Noah blinked. As much as he loved drawing, he hoped that wasn't the case.

Jeff picked up a notebook and shoved it at Noah. "Come on, Picasso. Let's see what you can do."

"Picasso was a painter," Noah said.

"Whatever."

Noah sat down, but Mika said, "I think you can use it when you want to. We just need to help you figure out how."

Noah smiled. *I hope so.* He stared at the page, biting the inside of his lip. He thought more about what to draw than about the ridiculous notion that he could disappear at will. But because of the cramped space in the tiny tent, he couldn't ignore his friends' gazes on him.

"Could you not do that, please?" Noah asked, tapping his pencil on the page.

"Don't stare at him," Mika said, leaning over toward Jeff. "Makes him nervous."

"Well, how are we supposed to see if he disappears?"

Mika grinned. "I may not get much of a signal here, but we have technology." She pulled out her phone.

With his friends no longer staring, Noah focused on the page, his mind, and what he wanted to draw. As he had experienced countless times, the buzzing in his head increased. He sharpened it, focusing on what he wanted to draw—to will into existence on the page. With the three of them there, there was only one thing he could think of.

"There," Noah said, exhaling.

Between Noah's small hands, he held the best drawing he'd ever done. It was a picture of the three of them standing together. Noah stood in the center between his two taller friends. Jeff held bunny ears over Noah's afro, and Mika stuck out her tongue and gave the peace sign. The detail Noah had captured impressed even him. It was a picture he would hang.

The shadows had deepened, especially around Jeff's eyes. His leather jacket looked worn and one size too small for him. The tiny bumps on Mika's tongue were visible. Noah had once heard the expression "laughter is in the eyes," and her eyes twinkled in the drawing.

He turned around, and his friends stared at him with their mouths open. Mika pointed her phone at him, but their eyes were glazed. It was like they were staring right through him.

"Hey, guys!" Noah said, waving his hand in front of them.

"Oh. Sorry, buddy," Jeff said. "Forgot you were there. Did you get it?"

Mika nodded.

As she showed Jeff the video, Noah exhaled, wiping the sweat from his forehead and slumping against the tent's wall. *I'm so tired.* Yet he smiled at the sketch. It was still the best work he had ever done, and it was well worth it.

"Wow," Jeff said, peeking over the phone at Noah. "You really can disappear. You wanna see?"

"I'm good," Noah said. Jeff didn't even glance at the sketch. Judging from the expression on his friend's face, he knew that Mika hadn't faked the video. He wished it were a hoax. He had no idea what his disappearing meant.

"You know, I kinda just forgot about you," Jeff said. "And you're hard to forget with that massive hair of yours."

Noah lifted his tired head and smiled.

"That's beautiful," Mika said and gasped. She snatched the picture from Noah's hand, careful not to tear it. "Oh wow. You have a real talent."

"I can not only disappear but I can draw."

"I'm serious. It's fantastic." Her green eyes widened as she stared at the drawing.

"Thank...you."

"His drawings are always great," Jeff said, still staring at the phone. "Now let's get back to this disappearing business." His gaze went back and forth between Noah and Mika's phone. "What does this mean?"

Noah shrugged. "Don't look at me. I have no idea."

"Now that we've confirmed he can vanish," Mika said, "we need to test his abilities."

Noah squirmed on the tent's floor. "I have a feeling I'm not going to like this."

Mika and Jeff shared a smile.

CHAPTER 6

ON THE FOLLOWING weekend, the trio met back at Noah's hideout. Noah was the last one to arrive. He thought about not showing up but couldn't do that to his friends. He had barely drawn all week, afraid to disappear again. What if someone saw him? What would they think of him? He didn't dare practice trying to disappear on his own. He was too nervous about what might happen, and things were easier with the support of his friends.

Noah dragged his feet through the dirt and weeds, walking to them. He had thought about what was going to happen many times, and he still wasn't sure how it would all work out. Would he fade from existence? More importantly, what would his friends think of him?

Yet when he got to them, he didn't see judgment or fear in their eyes. He saw something else, and that did scare him.

Excitement.

Mika had brought her laptop and a backpack full of snacks. She had crackers, granola bars, bottled water, chips, and cookies.

"Jesus, Mika," Jeff said, digging through her backpack. "Do you think we're going camping?"

She shrugged. "My mom's always talking about going on a diet, so none of this will be missed. And yet in a month she will buy it all again. And it looks like Noah needs to restock the food with the three of us hanging out here." She snatched her bag away. "Will you slow down? We don't know how long this will take. This food needs to last."

"Mmm-okay," Jeff said through his mouthful of food.

"How do you want to do this?" Noah said, staring at his shuffling feet.

"Hey, listen," Mika said, cupping her fingers under Noah's chin, forcing him to meet her eyes. "It's going to be OK. We'll be with you every step of the way."

Noah nodded, breathing easier.

"Yeah, I wouldn't let anything happen to you," Jeff said, taking a bite of a cookie. "Who would I talk to in Mr. Hill's class?"

"So what should I do?" Noah asked, looking at his friends. "Draw again?"

"Hmmm, I've been thinking about that," she said, sitting on the log. "Every time you've used your powers, you've been drawing, correct?"

"I think so."

"So just pretend you're drawing without actually drawing." She paused. "Does that make sense?"

"Kinda. How do I do that?"

"I'm not sure," Mika said and shrugged. I don't draw. I'm a logical thinker and need data. Least that's what the counselor at my last school said. You're far more creative than me. Imagine you are drawing without actually drawing. Make sense?"

No. But Noah sat down on the ground, leaning against the fallen log. He had drawn hundreds of pictures and had probably thought about it thousands of times, but he had never pretended to draw before. But Mika was right. He had to learn how to disappear without drawing, and this was the first step.

Noah stared at the ground. Black ants crawled along it, and he twisted his body to avoid them. He made a note to clean up after Jeff's mess. Noah tried to draw it with his mind, thinking about the parts of the ant he would draw first, and how he would use the pencil to shade and darken in certain areas.

After a few minutes, Noah opened his eyes and said, "Well?"

"Sorry, buddy," Jeff said, "Nothing happened."

"Nothing?"

"Nothing," Mika said. She paced in front of him. "Maybe we're doing this all wrong. My mom was real big into yoga for a time. She said the most important thing was breathing. Are you breathing correctly?"

Noah shrugged. "I don't know. I thought about how I would draw like I normally do."

"I think we're going about this all wrong," Jeff said, munching on a cracker. "Noah, I've known you your whole life, and I've seen you draw since I can remember. You once told me the reason you did it was because you felt bored and also trapped. Instead of thinking about the technical side of drawing, maybe you need to think about the way you *feel* when you draw."

"Huh," Noah said, scratching his head.

"And when you do it," Mika said. "This time try to be aware of us. Sneak up on us or something. Don't get lost in your disappearance."

Noah nodded.

He closed his eyes again. This time not to think of the ants beneath his feet. He thought of the way numbers made his head hurt. How Mr. Hill's deep voice droned on and on during class. How Noah never seemed to fit in with the other kids and how alone he felt during and outside of class. There was only one time when he didn't feel that way in school—when he drew.

The pressure and buzzing in his head increased. Aching to draw, he glanced around for a pen and paper. There was one just inside the tent. He went to get it then stopped. *That's not the point of this.*

Noah held that aching feeling inside his mind. The pain flooded throughout his body. It needed a release, and drawing was normally that release.

"Guys?" Noah asked, looking at his two friends.

"Noah?" Jeff asked.

They stared through him instead of at him.

Noah got up and crept around them. The crunchy noise of the dry grass and weeds caused his friends to turn his way. He softened his footsteps, and he couldn't help but grin when the pair struggled to find him.

"Boo!" Noah yelled as he reached out and grabbed Mika's back from behind.

She yelped before turning around and slapping him in the face.

"Ow!" Noah fell to the ground, rubbing the side of his face and rematerializing in front of them.

Mika towered over him. "Don't ever do that again!"

"OK, I'm sorry. But did you have to hit me so hard?"

She reached out and helped him up. "Sorry, but I don't like being scared."

"Well, did it work?" Noah asked.

"You bet it did!" Jeff said. "One second you're in front of us, then poof—the next you're gone." He scratched his head. "I still don't get it. I was watching you and then you weren't there. But I don't remember seeing it."

"Me neither," Mika said. "It's like...it's like I forgot you were even there."

"Definitely not like the movies," Jeff said. "How do you feel buddy? You all right?"

Noah held the fallen trunk for balance. "I'm good, but my head's a little sore and not from where Mika hit me."

"Maybe we should slow down. In time, it should be easier. We don't want you to push yourself too hard. We still don't know what you can do."

Noah shook his head. "That's why we're doing this. I want to learn more."

Mika smiled. "Then let's see what you can do."

Noah's feet grew heavier with every step he took. He stopped in front of his house, wiping the sweat from his head and gulping down the last of his bottled water. Smiling in relief, he made his way home. And just in time too. The sun had an hour at most before it disappeared for the night.

The garage was open and a beat-up old Mustang was inside with a familiar figure looming underneath its hood.

"Hi, son," Dad said, peeking out from his work before ducking his head back in. "You've been out all day."

"Yeah, was Mom worried?"

"No more than normal. Can you hand me a half-inch socket wrench?" Dad stuck his hand out.

Noah glanced at his dad's work bench seeing everything, including wrenches, hammers, screwdrivers, and things he didn't know what they were called. His dad's hand waved in the air.

"Ummm...this one?" Noah grabbed the nearest tool lying near him and handed it to his dad.

His dad finally poked his head out from under the hood and frowned. "Close. This is a crescent wrench because..." Dad raised his eyebrows.

Noah stared at the wrench, struggling to even see it. It had been a very long day, and all he wanted was to curl up in his bed, lay his head on the pillow, and close his eyes.

"A moon wrench?"

Dad smiled and chuckled. "Close enough. Personally, I like that name better. I need the wrench that makes your favorite sound."

Noah's eyes widened. "Oh! He rushed to the work bench, grabbing the correct tool. This one. Er-er-er," Noah said, mimicking the wrench.

His father laughed. "Thanks. Glad to see you go outside more. What's this I hear about a new girl?"

Noah rolled his eyes, wishing that his mom didn't know about Mika. Moms could be so embarrassing.

"Dad. She's just a friend. Me and Jeff are just showing her around, that's all. She doesn't have any other friends. Thank God she's not like Tricia or Lainey. Mika's...different. She's very smart and has black hair."

Dad had a wry smile on his face. "Different, huh? You'll have to tell me all about her."

Noah squinted and grunted in suspicion. "Dad, what did Mom tell you?"

"Nothing much. You should invite her over for dinner sometime. Women love that."

"She's just a friend."

His father grinned but ducked his head back under the hood. "If you say so. I'm glad you're showing this new girl around. It's thoughtful of you. You know you need to help people when you can."

Noah rolled his eyes, having heard that a million times. "I know, Dad."

Dad chuckled. "Just making sure. Want to help me?"

"Aww, Dad. You know I'm not interested in cars. I just don't understand them."

Dad poked his head out, and a pained look glimmered in his eyes. "This car is meant for you one day. I bought it when you were born to fix it up by the time you're old enough to get your license."

"I know, but I just don't get cars." He threw his hands up in frustration. "They're so loud and big. My feet won't even reach the pedals."

"They will when you get older."

"I can't even tell wrenches apart."

"Neither could I when I was your age," Dad said. "You love to draw. Just think of a car as a bunch of shapes put together. Maybe one day you'll change your mind." He poked his head back under the hood. "Go get washed up. Dinner's almost ready."

"OK." Noah sighed. He paused when he walked by his dad. *I wish we had more in common, and I wish I got cars.*

But he didn't think he ever would, especially now. There were far more important things than cars, or even drawing, on his mind.

He ran up the stairs to his room and changed out of his clothes. As he stared at his hands, Noah knew that life would never be the same again.

CHAPTER 7

THE ENTIRE weekend, Noah had practiced using his ability. He only finished his home-work because his parents made him and, unfortu-nately, he didn't get to draw at all. Yet because of all the practice, he was now able to disappear when he wanted to without drawing. And with each try, he was able to do it longer and more easily.

Noah didn't feel completely comfortable with disappearing. It was still so weird to move in a world where people couldn't see him. But that didn't stop Mika and Jeff from coming up with plans for him.

They wanted him to see the tests the teachers were giving out or, better yet, take the answers. Jeff thought that Noah could sneak into a video game store and take all the newest games. Or maybe even rob a bank if cameras couldn't see him.

But Noah wasn't a thief or a cheater. He was just a kid, and he wasn't going to do any of that.

He went along with testing his abilities because he wanted to find out more about them himself. For better or worse, his disappearing powers were a part of him. But there was something missing. He didn't know what to do with them.

Mika and Jeff wouldn't stop pestering him throughout the school day about doing something with his powers. That pair had so many ideas, and they wanted the tests to be—how had Mika put it?—in an uncontrolled environment. Noah had never been more thankful to hear the final bell ring.

The trio stood outside the classroom in the busy hall.

Noah leaned against the lockers as his friends discussed all the exploits they had planned for him. With no input from him. He perked up, remembering he could disappear. If he left now, he could slip away from them, maybe somewhere quiet to draw.

"We've already tested that Noah can't go through things," Jeff said.

"And that he's not captured on film," Mika said, cupping her chin. "Noah, what would you like to do?"

And that's the question. I wish I could just draw.

But his friends were right. These were his powers, and he needed to figure out what to do with them.

Before Noah could answer, he was slammed into nearby lockers. He yelped in pain as the lock dug into his arm. His books and papers spilled all over his half-opened backpack.

"Hey!" Mika said. "What a jerk!"

As she and Jeff scrambled to pick up Noah's belongings, Noah stared at the lumbering figure who had caused it.

Frank.

Frank turned around and grinned at Noah before stomping down the hallway.

Noah clenched his fists. Things were different now, and he made up his mind what to do.

"Noah?" Mika asked, glancing around, holding his papers and books in her arms. But in the spot Noah had stood was his open backpack.

Noah remained hidden and calm, stalking Frank as he left the school. He breathed like Mika's mom's yoga teacher had instructed her to do. *In. Out. Slow and steady.* He was thankful that he had left his backpack behind. The extra weight would have strained him even more.

All the extra work he and his friends had done had paid off. It was one thing disappearing in class and in and around the tent. It was another thing doing it while he was tracking someone with cars and other people to dodge.

He kept his steps small, keeping a respectful distance from Frank. He had to hurry to keep up with Frank's long strides. Frank led him east, away from the school and to a part of town where Noah didn't venture much.

The houses in Frank's neighborhood were more tightly packed together than those in Noah's neighborhood. The smaller yards had wild, uncut grass, and the cracks in the roads matched the ones in the sidewalk. Noah stared at a house sign, trying to read the name on it when a thick branch snapped under his weight and he froze.

Frank's lumbering body paused, turning around. Noah held his breath, not daring to meet Frank's eyes, afraid that he might see him there, even though that was impossible. Jeff and Mika had tried and they had never seen him. But what if Frank saw him? What if Noah lost his concentration or his powers faded?

Dead. Meat.

Frank stared at him, and the sweat dripped from Noah's body. *What if he can see me?*

Frank turned around and continued to walk. Noah's shaky legs wanted to collapse to the ground. He didn't, instead continuing his pursuit of Frank.

Frank's house was at the end of a block. A broken fence surrounded the single story house. The weeds leading to the front door were nearly as high as Noah. The paint was peeling and yellowing, and the front windows had large cracks in them and the screens were torn. The screen door slanted off the hinges.

"Jesus," Noah whispered.

Frank threw open the door, and Noah quickly followed on his heels, nearly slamming into the big bully.

Frank stomped off to his room and Noah stared at the mess in the house, afraid to move on the thick carpet. A large scratched living room table took up most of the space. Smelly clothes had piled up on the edge of the couch. Pictures of brightly colored flowers plastered the walls. In the middle of the wall, behind the couch, was a tattered print of a famous painting, and one he had seen before.

But where? That's it!

Noah vaguely remembered learning about it one time when his mom and dad took him to the museum in the city. He enjoyed the trip although he wished he could one day be as famous and as skilled as those artists. But there was this one painter—Edward some-thing. He was known for *The Scream* painting. But that painting wasn't in Frank's house. It was another one. It was the one with the woman with the red hair comforting the crying man.

Noah thought it odd at the time because it wasn't called *The Crying Man* or *Comforting Woman*. It had something to do with vampires, but it didn't look that way to Noah. The woman appeared to be caring for that man with her long, red hair draped over him.

Why is it here?

Frank had always mocked Noah's drawings. He didn't expect him to have any sort of artwork in his house aside from anime girls or comic books.

Frank had set his backpack down and run off. Noah shook his head. He knew he shouldn't have gotten absorbed in the painting. Now, wasn't the time for art. Now was the time for revenge.

But staring at the messy house, Noah had no idea what he was going to do. Maybe Noah could find some embarrassing pictures of Frank naked or on the toilet when he was a baby. For some reason, parents loved to take pictures like that.

Or maybe Noah should take something precious from him. Something from his childhood. That would be perfect revenge since as Frank took things that didn't belong to him, like Noah's drawings.

Noah crept through the small house, daring himself to breathe with each step. He turned the corner to the hallway and nearly ran into Frank. Noah quickly hugged himself against the wall, flattening himself as best he could.

"Come on, Grammy," Frank said. Noah held his breath as he passed by.

Frank guided an elderly woman from the hallway. "You can do it. Hold on." Frank rushed and cleared a pathway for her before setting her down at the kitchen table. "Let me give you your medicine."

She patted his hand. "Such a good boy."

Frank took her pills out of a container and measured the liquid with nimble hands before pouring it down her throat.

"Have a good day at school?" she asked.

He shrugged. "Just another day."

"When are you going to invite one of your friends over?"

Friends? When did Frank have any friends?

"You know how it is, Grammy. They're too busy, and I have to take care of you."

"You should be with kids your own age." She gently patted his face. "Not with an old woman all the time."

Frank helped her up. "Let's go get you cleaned up before I make you dinner."

"Good, good. Then I trust you'll do your homework."

"If I have time. I still have to clean up."

"Bah!" she said with a smile on her face. "Always with the excuses."

Frank returned the smile before bending down to kiss the small woman's forehead. Frank and his grandma passed by Noah and disappeared back into the hallway.

I can't do this. Noah thought. *This isn't right.* He left Frank's place and headed for home with a deep sadness and understanding of Frank.

When Noah arrived home, he found two familiar faces sitting around the dining room table along with his mother. Jeff and Mika ate freshly baked chocolate chip cookies.

"Shoes," Mom said.

"Sorry."

Noah hadn't expected to see his friends here, but at least they had his backpack. His mom told them to stay and clean up for dinner. When they went upstairs, Noah used that opportunity to fill his friends in on what had happened at Frank's.

"I can't believe it," Jeff said when Noah was finished. He put his fingers through his matted hair and leaned against the glass shower door. "I didn't think he had a kind bone anywhere in his body."

Mika crossed her arms. "It still doesn't give him the right to pick on you or anyone else."

"No, it doesn't," Noah said. "But I do understand him better. And going to his house made me realize what I want to do with my powers—what I *should* do with my powers."

Mika adjusted her glasses and blinked, her green eyes looming large. "Which is?"

"I want to help people."

Jeff leaned forward and grinned. "Should we make you a cape?"

CHAPTER 8

NOAH, MIKA, AND JEFF sat down at the lunch table, and Noah didn't get more than two bites of his peanut butter and jelly sandwich before his friends started bombarding him with questions and ideas like they normally did every chance they got.

"The Invisible Kid," Jeff said, leaning over.

"No," Noah said.

"Spooky Ghost."

"What? No."

"Afro-boy!"

Noah snorted.

"The Disappearing Act?"

"I kinda like that one," Mika said, waving her chicken finger around before eating it.

Noah took another bite of his sandwich. At times like this, he wished he had more friends, or people he could trust. He trusted his parents, but there was no way he could tell them something like this.

Maybe one day.

"If you don't like names," Jeff said. "What about a costume? We can always come up with a name later." He ate one of the cookies he had taken home with him last night. "Tell your mom I said thanks. I love these. Do you like capes? Capes are cool. But they're not practical and you can't fly."

Mika pushed up her glasses on her face. "First, we still don't know how his powers function, and what the limits of his abilities are. We need to continue with those tests. Everything else is superficial."

Mika and Jeff argued over what they thought Noah should do. He watched, doing his best to block out the noise and eat his food in peace. Noah knew what he wanted to do, but he couldn't figure out a way to do it. Some superheroes had the money to tap into police computers while others could swing from tall building to tall building and patrol the streets. He couldn't do any of that.

"Stop!" Noah yelled, putting a hand to his head. All the kids around the lunch table paused their conversations and stared at him.

"Freak," one of the kids said and they laughed.

"Hey!" Mika said, glaring at them. She and Jeff rose from the table.

Noah reached out and grabbed her hand. "Forget about them. It's not important. We have other things to think about."

The pair sat back down.

"OK," Jeff said, running his fingers through his hair.

"What's on your mind?" Mika asked.

"Simple. I want to help people. Let's start by doing that."

Mika and Jeff paused. Noah waited for their reactions and didn't say anything. He didn't care about stupid names or costumes. This wasn't a comic book. This was real life. And like his dad had taught him, "If you can, you help people."

"How?" Jeff asked, scratching his head.

"I was thinking we start small," Noah said. "But I'm open to ideas. Maybe I can make sure some of the students get their homework in on time or aren't late for class? Or finding lost pets? Or—"

"Spying on their older brother or sister!" Jeff said. He grinned. "I bet people will pay well for that."

"This isn't about money. And I don't want people to know it's me." He thought of his mom and dad. "It can get dangerous."

"That's why I think you should wear a costume."

Noah glared at him. "Jeff, this isn't a game."

"It's not," Mika said, shoving her half-eaten bag of chips at Jeff. "But we still don't know what you're fully capable of. That's why I think we need to do more tests. Take things nice and easy. That way there's no risk to you."

Noah sighed. "But I'm tired of tests."

Mika's eyes darkened. "You said it yourself. This isn't a game. If you don't know what you're doing or how far you can take your abilities, you or someone else could get hurt."

"That's why I wanted to start doing small things." Noah crossed his arms, not daring to meet her eyes. The lunch room was nearly empty now as most of the students had left to go play. The lunch staff picked up the dirty trays scattered around the room.

"Maybe we can do both," Mika said. "Like my mother says, 'It's not an either/or thing.' I'm never entirely sure what she means but it applies here. I think."

"Where do we start?" Jeff asked.

The school bell rang, but it was a sound Noah had heard only on occasion, and never in the middle of lunch. Both he and Jeff looked up at it. *That's not right.*

"That's odd," Mika said. "Don't we have like fifteen more minutes or something?"

"That's not the lunch bell," Noah said. He rose from the table and grabbed his bag. "Come on. We've got to get to the auditorium."

All the students in school fit into the auditorium, but just barely. The teachers had to stand in the aisles if there were no absences. And they had to stagger the school plays during the year.

The students sat with their classmates, among other students in their grade levels. The older kids were at the front, and the younger kids were at the back. The auditorium's seating slanted down so the younger kids could see. Noah, Jeff, and Mika, being in the fourth grade, were in the middle.

Noah leaned over to Mika. "Years ago, they had the younger kids in the front and the older kids in the back. That didn't work out too well. The bigger kids got rowdy and made snide remarks. A couple years ago they changed it."

Noah looked over his shoulder, remembering that he used to sit all the way up there. With each year as he got closer to the front, he became more nervous. He squirmed in his seat. *There's nothing like being the center of attention.* Good thing he could disappear.

She nodded. "What do you think it's about?"

"It's never good news," Jeff said, glancing around the room. "If it was some stupid announcement or guest speaker or something, we would have already known about it. It would have been on the calendar. It's something else. Whatever it is. We have bigger things to worry about." He elbowed Noah. "Right, buddy?"

"Right." But Noah wasn't convinced. Something was wrong here.

"I've noticed," Mika said, putting a finger to her chin but still staring at the stage, "that the more time passes and the more you use your powers, the easier it's getting for you."

Noah nodded. It *was* getting easier.

"I can't see what else you can do."

Noah chuckled. "Neither can I."

"Here she comes," Jeff said.

The heels of her shoes could be heard loudly as the principal walked onto the stage.

"Principal Reis," Jeff said.

But Noah wasn't paying attention to the principal. He spotted two uniformed police officers at the side of the stage.

With a glare from Principal Reis, the chattering died down. "Children, there has been a situation.

There's been a tragedy at the neighboring Clara Barton Junior High School." She raised her eyebrows. "There's currently a school shooting."

The kids in the auditorium started whispering until those whispers roared into a chorus. They had grown up with school shootings all across the country. One had happened two counties over. Unfortunately, there seemed to be one every month.

But they were lucky that none of them had taken place so close to where they lived...until now.

"Good thing we practiced those stupid school shooter drills," Jeff said, leaning closer to his friends. "I just wish we didn't have to use them. I hate hiding in closets."

"Me too," Mika said.

The police officers walked to the front of the stage.

"This is Officers Stern and Jones," Ms. Reis said. "Please give them your full attention."

The portly older one cleared his throat and straightened out his bushy mustache. "Students, due to today's unfortunate events, you will be indoors for the rest of the day." The kids groaned. "Hopefully, we will have cleared up the incident at Barton Junior High by the time school is over. But if not, me and Officer Jones will be patrolling the hallways until such a time arrives."

The younger officer smiled and waved to the kids.

"If you hear the school shooting bell, remember that it won't be a drill," Officer Stern said. "Follow your teacher's instructions, and we promise, we'll keep you safe."

The police officers stepped aside.

"If there are any more announcements, they'll be over the PA system," Principal Reis said. "Please go about your normal day and concentrate on your studies."

"That's going to be impossible," one of the students behind Noah said.

Agreed.

And yet what bothered Noah the most wasn't the school shooting itself. It was how it had become a part of life. The kids weren't even bothered by it, and the adults, with all their promises and grand gestures, didn't care.

Nothing's changed.

As Noah stared at the empty stage, Mika shook him hard. "Come on, let's get to class. It'll probably be a light rest of the day."

"Yeah," Jeff said. "Maybe we'll get lucky and watch a movie or something."

"I'm not going to class," Noah said.

"Yeah, right. Where are you going then? Home?"

Noah stood up, remembering the fear he'd felt when he learned of a school shooting one county over. How it was all over the news and then forgotten about in a week. The look of fear in the kids' faces as their classmates died. The weeping of parents whose kids were never coming home.

Noah was tired of seeing that all over this so-called great country. A great county wouldn't let their kids die.

"I'm not going home," he said, clenching his fists. He knew it was dangerous and foolish, but he had to try. Mika was right. He was getting stronger in his abilities.

"I'm going to Barton High, and I'm going to stop this."

Before they could stop him, he disappeared.

CHAPTER 9

NOAH PUSHED all his thoughts—all the noise—out of his head, clearing his mind as he did when he drew. He pulled himself out of the world and disappeared, crawling over the seat in front of him. His friends called out his name, but he didn't dare turn back.

Noah had to hurry. If the police were here that meant they were swarming Barton Junior High, waiting. Adults liked to wait. If Noah ran, he might make it in twenty minutes, but only if he pushed hard enough. Would he still be able to use his powers, or would he be out of breath by then? Noah bumped other students, but he had no time to waste. They thought it was the kid next to him, not realizing it was an invisible kid.

As he headed for the side doors, he mapped out the shortest distance to Barton Junior High. He was so busy that he didn't see the two police officers standing near the door. His feet skidded across the floor, and he barely stopped himself from crashing into them.

The older officer sighed. "I tell you, Jones, I can't wait to retire. This is not what I thought I'd be doing."

Jones nodded. "Neither did I."

"Back in my day, I used to love going to schools and educating kids on what we did. That was fun. I know some officers don't much care for it, but I felt like I made a difference in their world if only for a brief moment." He rubbed his hands to his face. "These days all I do is deliver news like this and do shooting drills. What kind of world is it we live in?"

"Come on," Jones said. "Let's go to the teacher's lounge and get you a coffee."

Stern rubbed his fingers through what was left of his hair. "I'm going to need something stronger than that. The kid's got hostages. I just pray that some of them will come home alive. I don't want to hear no more about *acceptable losses*. It's going to be a long day."

Hostages. Most of the school shootings were fast with a high body count. But if there were still hostages, that meant that Noah still had time to save them before it was too late.

When he reached the perimeter of Barton Junior High, he bent over, panting for breath. He had never run so fast and far before. The dripping sweat formed a puddle underneath him.

"Come on," Noah said to himself. He inhaled and straightened himself up. "You've got work to do."

Unlike his own school, Barton Junior High was on flat ground. It usually made it easier to get around, but today news anchors, concerned parents, and polic e officers crowded the perimeter. It wasn't the throng of people that bothered him, it was the shooter. *Where would he be?*

As Noah looked around the sea of people, he knew who would know. *The police!*

Noah didn't use his powers as he waded into the crowd. It had been tiring enough running all the way here, and he knew he'd need to save his powers for when it mattered. The crowd thickened. News reporters and concerned parents crowded against the police barricade, brushing up against him as he reached the barrier.

"Is my kid in there?" a mother asked. "You need to go in and rescue her before it's too late."

"Yeah!" a father said. "He's already killed three. We don't want any more of our kids to die. We know you have him cornered!"

"Get 'em outta here!" a policeman said. "Back! Back! You guys are getting in the way."

"We have a right!"

"Let us do our jobs and we'll bring the rest home safely."

One person grabbed Noah's arm and said, "Hey, you shouldn't be here!"

Noah pulled away from the woman and darted deeper into the crowd. As the mass of people swelled and pushed up against him, he knew he wouldn't be able to get any closer. As he ducked under the police tape, he let his mind and imagination leave his body as he did when he drew, turning invisible.

Noah passed by a couple of police officers talking to each other. They faces were looking at the crowd but one glanced over her shoulder.

"I always hate this part."

"The waiting? Yeah, me too." He took off his hat and ran his fingers through his thinning hair. "How much longer?"

She sighed. "Unfortunately, it won't be long now that we've got him cornered in the art room."

The art room. Noah slipped away from them. Noah had been to Clara Barton's art room for some event his parents thought he would like. He remembered being impressed by the older kids' drawings and he couldn't wait to go there so he could learn more from the teacher.

Police had scattered throughout the school, their walkie-talkies constantly going off as he went by. He didn't even need to know where the shooter was. The farther he went, the thicker the cops became, peering intently at the room he was headed toward.

Noah squeezed between two police officers walking by and spotted the classroom. Drawings were plastered all over the door and windows. A pink elephant raised its hind legs, and a beautiful sunset blossomed over a deep blue sea. There was even a skilled drawing of the popular cartoon with the robot monkey. It pained Noah that it had to take place in this class-room. He was hoping to come here in a few years, but now it would forever be tainted by this day.

The windows had been shut, so there was no way to see inside and only one way in. And that door had every trained cop focused on it and a crazed kid with a weapon on the other side.

An older cop spoke with a megaphone. "Robert...Bobby, please let go of the hostages and turn yourself in. If you do, I promise you will not be harmed and you will get to see your parents."

"LEAVE ME ALONE!" he shouted.

The uniformed cop walked back to a small group of cops in suits, and Noah inched in closer to the art room door to listen.

I need to hurry. Noah stared at the door. He had to do something. It was only a matter of time before the cops charged in. Whenever they did, there would be more casualties. He had been given the gift for a reason, and he was going to put a stop to this. But first, he had to get inside.

Noah snuck to the door and leaned against it. He heard voices but couldn't make out what was being said. He pressed his face against the glass. The blinds blocked out everything.

Noah knew what he had to do. "Here goes."

He wiped his sweaty hand before putting it on the door handle.

What if it's locked? Odds are Robert wouldn't have the key, but the teacher might. If the door was locked, Noah couldn't do anything except wait for an opening.

As quickly as he could, he turned the knob, breathing a sigh of relief. He gave himself just enough of an opening to squeeze inside. The old door creaked as it opened, and a kid not much older than Noah turned around. He held up the handgun.

"Who's that?" he said. "Don't come in! I warned you not to come in." He waved the gun around, pointing it at the door.

Noah froze, his eyes focused on the barrel of the gun fifteen feet from him. Robert ran toward the open door, and Noah barely got out of the way as Robert rushed by him, slamming the door shut.

"Why won't they leave me alone?" Bobby said. He put his hand to his head and pounded it. "It's so loud. Why is everyone so *loud?*"

Noah stared at the crowded kids in the corner. They were older than Noah, but didn't look that way now. They huddled against the slim teacher, tears running down their silent faces.

"Bobby," the teacher said. "No one's saying any-thing." The teacher rose from the kids and gingerly went to him.

Noah held his breath, wanting her to succeed. Maybe he wouldn't have to do anything. Maybe this teacher was good and she would reach him.

"Bobby," she said, "I've known you since you were a baby." She crept closer. "I used to babysit you for your mom. I bandaged your knee when you fell. We watched cartoons together." She smiled. "I even changed your diaper for Christ's sakes. Come on, Bobby, you know me."

The young teacher reached out to him, steadying her hand as she did so.

"No!" Bobby yelled, slapping her hand away, his gun pointing at her. "Get away. All of you need to be quiet, especially you, Ms. Green."

He's insane. I need to do something.

"Who's there?" Bobby spun around toward Noah.

Noah froze, not daring to move, breathe, or even blink. *He can't see me, can he?* No. That buzzing sensation Noah had when drawing was still there, and none of the other kids or the teacher had even looked his way. He was still invisible.

"I know you're there," Bobby said, pointing his gun in Noah's direction. But his eyes weren't looking at Noah. They darted around.

"Bobby," Ms. Green said. "There's no one else here."

"You don't understand, Ms. Green," he said, closing his eyes and breathing deeply. "No one understands! The noise. It's all I hear. It's all that's around me. Every day, no matter what I do. I can't shut it off!"

"What noise?" she asked.

"THE NOISE!" He banged his fist against his head. "And there's a new one here now."

The gunman inched closer and Noah tiptoed away from him. He stepped behind the teacher's desk and over a stack of fallen books. Yet everywhere Noah moved, Bobby seemed to track him. With the kids and teacher all huddled in the back of the classroom, Noah had more space to move, but it was only a matter of time before Bobby found him or, worse, fired the gun.

"Stop toying with me!" Bobby said. He fired the gun, one bullet after another in quick succession, yelling each time he pulled the trigger.

Noah hadn't even realized that he had closed his eyes. When he opened them, small holes were in the wall a couple of inches from where he stood.

Oh my God. Noah couldn't move. He had been inches from death. His friends were right. He shouldn't have come here. He was just a kid and he could have been killed! He looked to the door. *It's time for me to leave.*

"There's nothing there!" Ms. Green said. "What are you shooting at?"

Bobby spun around to face his teacher. "It's *there!*"

But Noah was no longer there. He had moved away from his spot, getting closer to freedom. With each step he breathed easier. All he had to do was leave and pray that Bobby wouldn't kill any more students.

Noah placed his hand on the door's handle. He sniffled and put his free hand to his nose. His finger came away with droplets of blood. Noah rubbed his temples and his vision blurred. He used the door handle for support. He had to get away and quickly. This was the longest he had used his powers. He wasn't sure how long he could maintain it.

"There's only one way I could focus on that noise I know is there," Bobby said, rubbing his temple with the muzzle of the gun. "It's to quiet the rest of you."

Bobby leveled the gun at his classmates and teacher. *No!*

Noah forgot about the pain in his body or even his own life. He ran toward Bobby, barreling into the gunman. A shot went off and wide as they tumbled and crashed to the ground, sending Bobby's gun sliding across the floor.

Noah screamed in pain as Bobby's weight had crushed his wrist. He lay on the floor, cradling it, the pounding in his head increasing. His loss of concentration was visible to the entire class.

"See!" Bobby yelled, pointing at Noah. "I told you! There *was* someone else here! I'm not crazy! I'm not crazy!"

Heavy, thunderous footsteps burst through the door. Armed SWAT officers rushed in with guns drawn.

"Don't shoot!" Ms. Green said, waving her hands as she stood in front of the children. "He's down!"

Bobby kept shouting and pointing at Noah. "See, he's there! I'm not crazy! I'm not crazy!"

Noah concentrated and faded before anyone else could see. But Bobby still stared at the spot Noah was, screaming like a madman as they dragged him away in handcuffs. Paramedics rushed him along.

Noah lifted his tired head, wiping the blood from his nose and cradling his sore wrist. Luckily, it wasn't the hand he drew with. All he wanted to do was rest. But Noah had to keep moving. He needed to get out of there. He still maintained control of his powers, but he wasn't sure for how long. He pushed himself off the floor but winced from the pain in his wrist. He leaned against a table for balance before scurrying out of the room.

Noah used the handrail for support as he made his way away from all the commotion. *Just a little further.* He squinted, making out the crowd and where his friends would be. He spotted the police officers he'd stood beside earlier and headed in that direction to get more information. A young man in a black suit with dark shades stood next to the officers.

Must be the FBI, like in one of my mom's shows.

Noah approached them but wouldn't stay long. He just wanted to find out if anyone else was hurt or needed help. He weaved between the throngs of people passing by, doing his best to dodge them. When he was thirty yards away, the man in the suit and sunglasses turned to Noah.

Noah froze.

He let out a breath, but continued to walk toward them, this time from another angle. But the man's head turned and followed Noah's trail. Noah circled around, still keeping his eyes on him. Wherever he went, the man's gaze followed.

He can see me!

A crowd of emergency workers walked in front of Noah. He crouched down, waddling close to the ground, until he ducked behind a garbage can. He breathed heavily, feeling the strain of using his powers, but he didn't dare stop now.

Noah peeked around the garbage can. The man looked around but didn't find Noah. He left with the officers and disappeared into the crowd. Noah waited until he was sure it was safe to move on.

As soon as he passed the police barrier, he stopped using his powers. With all the commotion, no one noticed him except for two familiar faces.

Jeff and Mika ran over to him. Noah's legs were wobbly and he was drenched with sweat.

Mika held him up. "Are you OK? We were worried about you."

Noah couldn't even get any words out. He held onto Mika and shook his head. *Water, and a nap. That's what he needed.*

"You idiot!" Jeff said. "What made you come all the way over here by yourself? Something could have happened to you, especially without me."

"Leave him alone," she said. "He's exhausted. Take your time." She smiled. "Relax. You did it. You saved the kids."

"No..." Noah gulped down air. He shook his head. "Something's...wrong."

The smile across Jeff's face vanished. "What is it? What's wrong?"

"I...I...was seen."

"Yeah, we heard that on the radio. Everyone thinks he's crazy enough as is and—"

Noah grabbed his friend by the collar. "No. I was *seen.*"

"By who?" Mika asked. "What happened?"

"Let's get out of here and I'll tell you. It's not safe here."

CHAPTER 10

AS THE TRIO RUSHED back to Noah's hideout within the trees, Noah's friends wouldn't stop bombarding him with questions. He didn't answer their questions. And not because they were in a hurry and his wrist was sore and his body ached. He couldn't get that agent's stare out of his mind.

They finally reached Noah's hideout, and once they were inside the tent, Noah peeked outside just to make sure they weren't being followed.

"OK, now can you finally tell us what's going on?" Jeff asked, plopping down to the ground.

And so Noah told them. He told them about the cops and how they were tired of all the shootings just like he was. He spoke of what happened with Bobby and how he botched that. Then he moved onto Agent Man.

While almost getting shot had been the scariest moment of Noah's young life, the way Agent Man had stared at him was even more unnerving. *No one should be able to see me.*

"Are you all right?" Mika asked, glancing at his wrist.

Noah stopped rubbing it. "I'm OK. Just hurt it when Bobby landed on it. It's sore but nothing's broken."

"Mika," Jeff said, opening a bag of chips. "Do you really think that man saw Noah? With all the commotion, he could have been looking at something else."

She shrugged. "I don't know...it's possible. We have a friend who can disappear at will."

"What do you think it means?" Noah asked.

"I think it's nothing," Jeff said, waving his hand. A sly grin spread across his face. "But what if it is something? What if he's a part of a secret government organization whose sole purpose is to hunt down people like you and cut them open, stealing their powers for the military? Or what if he's part of a race of aliens that have gone down to Earth to find kids with abilities, and will transport them to their home planet. Or maybe—"

"Stop!" Mika said, snatching the bag of chips from Jeff's hand. "It's not funny."

Noah's breathing slowed down, and he scratched his sweaty forearms. He hadn't thought about all that. What if there was something more to Agent Man?

"It'll be OK, Noah," Mika said, offering him some chips. "No matter what, we're here for you."

"Yeah, I was just joking, bud," Jeff said. "You know I got your back."

"Let's just play it safe for the next few days," she said. "Don't use your powers, and don't be a hero. Think you can manage that?" She squeezed his hand and he smiled, returning it.

Noah nodded. "Yeah, I can do that." He didn't want to admit it, but using his powers for so long and in such a dangerous situation had worn him out more than he had thought it would. He just wanted to rest.

"As long as there isn't another shooting," Jeff said.

Their smiles faded.

"Uh-oh," Jeff said, looking at his phone. "School's out." He stood up. "We should get going. Our parents, even mine, will check in on us because of the shooting. I'll see you guys tomorrow."

"Think we'll get in trouble for cutting?" Mika asked.

"Nah," Noah said. "They have bigger problems. The worst part will be the week afterwards, with the counseling." He sighed. "I just hope I never have to see that man again."

"You're not alone," Mika said.

As Noah stared into her eyes, he realized that, while he might be a freak with a weird power, he wasn't alone. He always had Jeff and now Mika.

"Thanks."

Noah took his time in getting home. He needed time to think and he was so exhausted. His feet were dragging and his legs were heavy. *I don't know what worries me more: the school shooting or Agent Man.*

It was a struggle to find the right key to fit in the lock. He didn't even need to. The door opened and his mom and dad stood there. Dad rarely came home early. They grabbed him and he melted into their arms, squeezing them.

"We were so worried about you," Mom said into his ear.

Dad rubbed Noah's head. "Yeah, sport. It's why I came home early."

Tears ran down Noah's cheeks as he looked up at them. He knew they were worried about the school shooting, but there was so much more than that. He wanted to tell them everything. He wanted to tell them about his powers. How he had been foolish enough to go to the school to help them. He wanted to tell them everything. But he knew he couldn't.

Noah sniffled, wiping his tears and boogers on his mom's sleeve. "I'm good."

"Are you sure? We're here for you."

"Yeah. It's just...it's just been a very long day, and I'm tired."

"Go wash up," Mom said. "Dinner will be ready soon."

"Thanks, Mom."

As hungry as he was, he didn't wash up. As soon as he got to his room and saw his bed, he dragged his feet to it. He collapsed face first into the bed with thoughts of gunfire and fear to haunt his dreams.

CHAPTER 11

A WEEK HAD passed since the Clara Barton shooting. With the exception of all the reporters, the assemblies, the announcements, and the therapists, school was almost starting to feel normal. Almost.

Noah had just gotten out of his session with the school's therapist. He had said everything he was expected to say and talked about his feelings. But how did he really feel about his role in the incident? The sad thing was it wasn't like he'd had experience with this kind of thing. But it was the first time he had been actively involved in a shooting, and he had stopped it. Not that he'd told her about it.

Noah walked down the hall, relieved to get out of there. He adjusted the strap on his heavy backpack and gasped and stopped in his tracks. Frank stepped out of the room next door with the other therapist. A light sheen of sweat glistened off him, and he sniffled.

Did he cry? That's impossible. Frank never cries.

Frank stiffened when he saw Noah, and that familiar, malicious grin spread across his face.

Great. But instead of going down another hall to avoid him and run away, Noah continued walking straight toward Frank, although he did look at the ground, avoiding eye contact. No reason to provoke him.

Noah braced himself as Frank predictably bumped into him.

"Watch it, squirt!" Frank said.

"Sorry, didn't see you."

"You can't see anyone with that hair of yours." Frank paused. "Did you just see the therapist? Say, I bet she got you to cry. Did you cry?" Frank bent down until his face was right in front of Noah's.

Noah was right. He could clearly see the redness in Frank's eyes.

Noah thought about using his power to disappear. He wouldn't do that. This time he would face his problems.

"No, I didn't cry," Noah said. "But I wanted to. The things Ms. Miller said, reminded me of my grandma who passed away a few years ago."

Frank stepped back, clenching his fists. "What?"

"My grandma said that back in her day, all she had to worry about was homework, roughhousing boys, backstabbing girls, and rides home from strangers." Noah lowered his head. "She felt sorry for us because we have to worry about being shot in our own schools and that we're inheriting a world on the verge of col-lapse."

"My grammy says the same thing," Frank said.

Noah looked up into Frank's eyes. "I'm hoping to prove her wrong."

Frank stalked to Noah. Noah's body tightened and his shoulders crunched up, but he kept his eyes open. He would disappear if he had to, but he wasn't going to be afraid of Frank anymore. Not after last week's school shooting, and not after what he had seen at Frank's house.

Frank glared down at Noah. He snorted before pushing past Noah. "Yeah, right."

Whew.

As Noah watched Frank go, he realized that was the scariest thing he had ever done. More scary than facing down a school shooter. And he realized that he didn't need to actively stop people like he was a superhero. He could use his "superpower" to observe people and get to know them in ways they wouldn't reveal if they knew someone was watching.

With a smile on his face, Noah went back to Mr. Hill's class and sat down.

"How'd it go?" Jeff asked.

Noah shrugged. "The usual. But I ran into Frank coming out of it. You wouldn't believe what just happened. He—"

Noah froze.

"What is it?" Mika asked. She and Jeff followed his gaze, and Noah barely got the words out of his dry mouth.

"It's...him!"

The man Noah had seen at Clara Barton walked into the classroom with a piece of paper in his hands.

"Sorry to interrupt, Mr. Hill," he said. "But Ms. Reis wanted me to get started, and I chose your class first."

Noah dug his fingernails into the hardwood table, his palms so sweaty they left marks on them.

"Class," Mr. Hill said, peering down at the piece of paper. "This is Mr. Cooper. He is going to be at the school for the remainder of the day."

Noah held his breath as his heart nearly stopped.

"Thank you, Mr. Hill," Mr. Cooper said, smiling at the class. "Sorry to intrude, children, and right before lunch too. I wish I were here under better circumstances. But due to the tragedy at your neighboring school, I've come here to prepare you in case something like it happens again."

Mr. Cooper clapped his hands together. "Children, you've been drilled on what to do when one of your classmates makes the unfortunate and tragic decision to take someone else's life. But you need to remember that it's not your fault. There's nothing you can do about it. All you should do is be safe and let a responsible adult take charge of the situation. Don't be a hero."

Noah stiffened as Mr. Cooper's gaze rested on him for a second. But the man turned away, continuing to talk to the rest of the class.

"Sometimes you'll get in the way, and you can get yourself or others hurt."

Mr. Cooper opened his mouth to say more but glanced at the clock. "Guess that's it for today. Sorry I came so late Mr. Hill. I had exercises to do with the class ways that kids could spot a troubled youth and warn an adult. I guess I came too late."

Noah sat straight up, tense like a cat, ready to leave if the strange man tried something. He ached to disappear and bolt out the door, but if he did, what would the man do?

As the man spoke, he glanced at Noah but only like any teacher would do. His gaze didn't linger any longer than normal. "Thank you for your time." Mr.

Cooper shook Mr. Hill's hand before walking out of the room.

"See," Jeff whispered into Noah's ear. "You have nothing to worry about. Mr. Cooper is just one of those city counselors or something. Just to make sure the school doesn't get sued."

"Yeah," Mika said, leaning over. "Maybe he's right. I've seen a bunch of those types at all the schools I've been at." She rolled her eyes. "The things they have us do never works."

But as Noah stared at the door, he wasn't buying it. He needed to find out more about this Mr. Cooper, and he knew exactly how to do so.

When the lunch bell rang, Noah rushed out of the room with Jeff and Mika following on his heels.

"What do you plan to do?" Mika asked.

Jeff looked in the direction all the other kids were going. "Yeah, because I'm hungry. Can we, like, do it after we eat?"

"Come on," Noah said, grabbing Jeff and Mika. He gripped their clothes, creating a wall on either side of him. The good news was that, since Noah was so small, he could barely be seen. He was worried that Mr. Cooper might be in the hall. The bad news was that his gigantic hair made him stand out despite the size difference.

When he didn't see Mr. Cooper anywhere, Noah felt relaxed enough to walk from between his two friends, pausing at the corner of the hallway.

"So what'd you have in mind?" Jeff asked.

Mika squinted at him. "You're not planning on running away again, are you?"

"Nope. Not this time." He peeked around the corner. "I say we follow Mr. Cooper."

"But what if he can see you like you said?" Mika asked.

"I don't plan on using my powers."

Jeff grinned. "Good idea. No matter who he is he doesn't know the school better than us."

Noah and Jeff led Mika to where they thought Mr. Cooper would be during lunch—in the teacher's lounge.

The three kids easily made it to the lounge. The rest of the students were either in the cafeteria or on the playground. A few students were scattered through the halls or huddling on stairwells. The kids scanned the hallway, looking for any teachers going into the lounge. They didn't see any, so they thought it safe to go in.

"Come on," Jeff said, creeping to the door. Jeff and Mika peeked through the window.

"He's here," Mika whispered.

"What's he doing?" Noah asked.

She squinted. "He's reaching into his bag and he's pulling out some kind of device." She gasped. "It looks like he's taking the brains of the teachers!"

"I knew it!"

Noah tried to reach up to see, but Jeff pushed him back. "Down, or they'll see you."

"But—"

"Mika was just joking. They're just talking about...whatever boring things adults talk about."

"Wish we could hear them," Mika said.

Jeff ducked back down. "Come on, we can. I know a place."

"Oh yeah, that's right," Noah said.

Jeff ran down the hallway and Noah followed him.

"Wait!" Mika said. "Where are we going?"

The boys turned the corner of the teacher's lounge and went into the boy's bathroom.

Mika paused. Noah came back and pulled her inside.

"Huh?" A young boy said as he finished zipping up his pants. "What's she doing in here?"

"Beat it, Francisco," Jeff said, pointing his thumb at the door.

"Don't mind me," Mika said, strolling up to Francisco. "I just came to use the urinal like all nonbinary people."

Francisco rolled his eyes as he went to the sink.

"Out!" Jeff said, pushing him to the door. "Out!"

"But I didn't get to wash my hands."

"I'll tell your mom when you die of E. coli." Jeff pushed Francisco out the door and scurried to another door on the other side of the stalls. "Come on. We don't have much time. You know how adults are. They're always in a rush."

Jeff searched the white tiles on the bathroom floor near the door.

"What is he doing?" Mika asked.

"This bathroom and the janitor's closet are right behind the teacher's lounge," Noah said. "If we can get in, there's holes in the closet that we can peek and hear through. We'll just have to be quiet while we're in there."

"Yeah, some of the students use it to spy on them so we can get a head's up," Jeff said. "A-ha, gotcha!" Jeff pulled a piece of the broken tile away from the floor.

Jeff used that tile to bypass the lock on the old door and pry it open. "It's going to be tight for all of us." He motioned for them to go into the closet.

Noah wrinkled his nose at the chlorine smell and squeezed between his friends' legs. The three of them smushed together in the confined space before closing the door. The only light shone through the holes into the teacher's lounge.

As his taller friends squirmed and adjusted to the tight fit, Noah used his lack of height to squat down, peeking through the bottom hole. He blinked, allow-ing his eyes to focus on the numerous shapes. He couldn't see much from his low vantage point, but he could hear them.

"Why does the government insist on doing these little demonstrations?" Mr. Hill asked. "We all know it's meaningless? What we need is more security!"

Mrs. Chan rolled her eyes. "There you go again with that security nonsense. Metal detectors at every entrance and armed guards patrolling the halls."

"Well, why the hell not? It'd deter them from bringing guns in the first place."

"Sure, for like the first week," Mr. Bailey said. He took a bite of his sandwich. But the schools don't want to pay for it anymore, and remember that one school out west? He was able to get through their security and took, what, ten lives, including the armed guards."

"It would be better if the cause was treated, instead of the symptoms," Ms. Vera said.

"My sentiments exactly," Mr. Cooper said, smiling as he reached for more coffee. "We've been trying to work on that. There are a lot of troubled students and not enough teachers or therapists to go around. A lot of heads have been working on that problem around the clock."

Mr. Bailey rubbed the bridge of his nose. "Getting rid of the guns would help."

"Oh, not this again," Mr. Hill said, setting his coffee mug down. "First the students and now you. It's no wonder. You're about the same age as them. I'll never understand the nonsense you spout about getting rid of the guns. That won't solve the problem."

"But it'll help. Other countries—"

"Gentlemen, enough." Mr. Cooper said. He gave the teachers another warm smile that disarmed them. To Noah, it wasn't inviting at all.

"Unfortunately, neither you nor I make the policies," Mr. Cooper said. "That's for the people in - office." His hand reached for the pink box, but then stopped himself.

"Then why are you here?" Ms. Vera asked.

"My dear teacher, I'm here because we have something new in mind to curb unfortunate incidents like the school shooting." Mr. Cooper leaned forward and

Ms. Vera backed away. "It's still in its earliest stages, but we've come up with ways to ID high-risk targets. We've already implemented the program in a few select spots across the nation. One day, we hope to take it worldwide."

"I wish you had done it sooner," Mrs. Chan said. "Then maybe poor innocent kids wouldn't have been killed."

He sighed. "So do I. So do I." He perked up. "On the bright side, the reason I've come to this school is that there's a person of note here."

Mr. Bailey gasped. "You think there's a shooter here? At this school?"

"No, sorry," Mr. Cooper said, shaking his head. "The program we're working on can possibly identify a shooter, but it also can identify individuals of note who could be beneficial to society and even help us in stopping shooters. Unfortunately, that's all I'm allowed to say."

"Who of note could possibly be at this school for Christ sakes?" Mr. Hill said. "In all my years of teaching, I've never seen the students here amount to much."

"Blame the teacher, not the student," Mrs. Chan said, wagging her finger at him. All the other teachers in the room chuckled. Mr. Hill folded his arms.

"The program isn't perfect," Mr. Cooper said. "We're still working out a few of the bugs. But you'd be surprised who is special. In fact…"

"Will you scoot over?" Mika said, squirming in the janitor's closet.

"I'm sorry," Jeff said, trying to move around in the limited space. "I—"

Mika yelped as Jeff came into contact with her. She elbowed him, and he grunted in pain.

"Do you guys hear that?" Mr. Cooper asked.

The trio froze, no longer concerned with inappropriate touching, accidental or otherwise. Mr. Cooper stared at the wall they hid behind.

Noah held his breath as he didn't move and didn't dare blink. While the hole he stared through was small, it could be noticeable if one was looking for it. And Mr. Cooper was certainly looking for it.

"What do you hear?" Ms. Vera asked.

"I'm not sure." He inched his way closer to the thin wall and sweat dripped down Noah's forehead.

Noah scurried backward, tugging on his friends' legs. It was time to go. Whatever else Mr. Cooper was going to say, they wouldn't get to hear it.

The trio tumbled out of the closet, hurrying to carefully place everything where it had been before.

"Whew," Jeff said, wiping his forehead. "That was close."

Mika slapped Jeff. "Don't ever touch me like that again!"

"Ow!" He rubbed his red cheek. "I told you I was sorry. It was an accident. I didn't mean nothing by it. Swear."

Mika pushed her glasses up her nose, glaring at him. "All right. I believe you...this time."

A loud noise through the hall made Noah jump. It sounded like a large door being slammed. It could have been a kid, they'd slammed enough doors at Susan Anderson Elementary School, but kids wouldn't have slammed a door during lunch.

"Let's get outta here," Noah said, heading toward the door before one of the teachers found them in there. Or worse yet, Mr. Cooper.

Noah itched to use his powers and spy on Mr. Cooper some more, but he didn't dare do it. The most they did for the rest of the day was spy on him during recess. But they didn't learn anything more about him that day. They didn't even see him go anywhere near Mr. Hill's classroom again. He just went from classroom to classroom going about his job. Jeff and Mika were relieved, but Noah wasn't convinced.

After school, the trio walked home together like they normally did.

"Cheer up, Noah," Jeff said. "Tomorrow we'll find out more about him."

Noah put his hands in his pockets. "He'll be gone by then." He wasn't sure if that bothered him or if he was relieved.

Jeff wrapped his arm around his friend. "Doesn't matter. He may be gone but whatever information the teachers wrote down about him won't be. You can use your powers again."

"And I'll find out what they stored on the computers about him," Mika said. "I just need you to get me in there."

Noah perked up. His friends were right. They had a plan, and things would be easier without Mr. Cooper there. The way Mr. Cooper had stared at Noah unnerved him. And it wasn't just the fact that he could see him when he shouldn't be able to. It was that he didn't seem surprised by a disappearing kid.

Thankfully, he didn't have to think about Mr. Cooper now. With the week winding down and, unfortunately, another school shooting taking place across the country, things could finally get back to normal. As much as normal was for Noah these days.

Noah waved goodbye to his friends, looking forward to the weekend again. When he arrived home, both his parents were there. He shrugged, seeing new, nicer, cleaner shoes by the door. They were always buying shoes, especially his mom.

Hearing voices, he walked into the living room. He was about to greet his parents when he froze. Sitting on the couch were two strangers—including one who he had seen before.

Noah put a hand to his mouth then whispered, "Mr. Cooper."

CHAPTER 12

NOAH COULDN'T believe it. Mr. Cooper was here—in his living room! He had to do something. He had to disappear, runaway, anything!

"Noah, dear..." Mom's voice was far too calm. Didn't she see what was happening? She rose from the couch. "Just in time. This is Mr. Cooper and Ms. Luna. They've come to see you." His mom had a delighted smile on her face, but she couldn't—didn't—possibly know about what was going on.

Jeff was right. They had come to take him away to cut him up and find out what made him tick.

Mr. Cooper smiled. "A pleasure, Noah. We've already met at school. Under unfortunate circumstances, I'm afraid. This is my lovely assistant."

Ms. Luna smiled, but it lacked any sort of warmth. The thin woman with icy blonde hair stared at Noah with shrewd eyes.

"Noah," Dad said, "Don't be rude. Say hello."

But Noah couldn't say hello. He couldn't move at all. He hadn't expected this to happen. Not today. Not now.

Noah took a shaky step back. He would disappear and run away. He'd have to come back for his parents later, hoping they wouldn't freak over what they were about to see.

Mr. Cooper's smile faded and his voice snapped. "Stop!" He leaned forward, and Noah leaned back. "Noah, I can see that you're about to disappear again. I would advise you to stop. It would be a very foolish thing to do right now."

The thumping in Noah's chest intensified. He glanced at his parents' faces to see their reactions. They didn't move. They still had those same friendly faces.

"Mom? Dad?" Noah gently put his hand on his mom's shoulder, but she didn't even react, as if he weren't there.

"I wouldn't waste my time if I were you," Mr. Cooper said. "They can't hear you. Actually, that's not entirely accurate."

"What did you do to them?" Noah said, clenching his fists.

"If you promise to sit down and behave, I'll tell you. I promise you that no harm will come to your parents. I rather like your parents. They're good people."

Noah couldn't trust him. But as he looked back at his parents, he realized he didn't have a choice in the matter. He squeezed in next to his mom on the couch.

"I know this seems like a lot for someone your age," Mr. Cooper said. "But you're not the only one in the world with a gift. Ms. Luna here also has an ability." He gestured to her. She grunted, not looking at Noah. "Her ability is to slow down time like she did with your parents."

Even the hands on the clock in the living room moved more slowly. Outside, cars sped down the street, and one of the neighbors jogged down the side-walk. *There are limits to her powers.*

"Could we speed this up?" Ms. Luna asked, beads of sweat dripping down her temple.

"I was getting to that," Mr. Cooper said. "Noah, there's a place in the city that I'd like for you to see."

"I knew it!" Noah said, jumping to his feet. "You want to put me away and lock me up or cut me open!"

Mr. Cooper chuckled while Ms. Luna rolled her icy blue eyes. "Not at all. There's a school in the city that I'd like for you to be a part of. Gwyneth here was once a student. There, she learned about her abilities and how to control them. You can learn the same things she did with other people like you."

Noah held his breath. He would love nothing more than to understand his disappearing act. He glanced down at his hands. There was still much more he didn't understand about himself, and this would be the perfect opportunity to learn.

He looked to his parents to see what they would think. That's when Noah remembered that, because of Ms. Luna's powers, he couldn't. He couldn't even tell them what he could do.

Noah shook his head. "No thanks. I don't believe I'm ready for a place like that."

Mr. Cooper frowned. "That is a shame. But you're wrong. You're more than ready. And unfortunately, you don't have a choice. You're just a kid."

Before Noah could ask what he meant, Ms. Luna released the hold on Noah's parents.

"Noah," Mom said, squeezing her son's leg. "We're so excited for you. Mr. Cooper was telling us about a special school."

"Emma," Dad said, nudging her. "Not special. Gifted. Gifted school. Mr. Cooper was just telling us that you'd be perfect for it."

Noah glared at Mr. Cooper and crossed his arms. "My grades aren't good enough to get into a school like that."

"He didn't say anything about your grades. It was your art." Dad smiled. "See honey, I told you our son could be a famous artist."

"But what if I don't want to go to a new school? I like the one I'm at now."

"Then you won't have to," Mom said. "But we'd at least like to check it out. Isn't that right, Mr. Cooper?"

Mr. Cooper gave his patented smile, but Noah didn't like the look of it. "Of course. We'll be in contact." He rose, heading for the door. "I can't wait for young Noah to see our school. I think he'll love it there."

Try as he might, he couldn't convince his parents to not take him to visit the school. They thought it was a great opportunity especially his mom. And Jeff and Mika weren't any help either. Whether or not Noah was going to go to the school, they thought it a great opportunity to spy while he was there.

Since Noah wasn't getting out of visiting the school, he might as well accept the mission his friends had laid out for him. Try to find out as much information as he could. Talk to the students and see their abilities. And when he got home, tell his friends all about it. *Assuming they don't mind wipe me when I leave.*

Noah crossed his arms and stared out the window, ignoring his parents in the front seat. Their words about how exciting it was for him and how it was a good opportunity for him and that they'd never had a chance like this went through Noah's head on the long car drive. Normally, Noah would be asleep on the thirty-minute trip to the city, forty-five with traffic. But he was too nervous today.

"Where are we going?" Noah asked, sitting up. When, they went to the city, it was usually downtown, to a restaurant, or to the park. This wasn't a part of the city he was familiar with.

"You missed it," Dad said, glancing back at his son as he drove. "But Mr. Cooper said they hope to find a bigger place for the school one day."

Noah's parents took him to a part of the city he hadn't been to—the industrial section. Since it was the weekend, most of the buildings were closed. The commercial trucks were idle, and all the big trucks that would be delivering and receiving were gone.

There was plenty of parking. And there were plenty of homeless people, with their tents and RVs providing a semblance of a home. Noah frowned. He'd once asked his parents about that, and they'd said that things had gotten worse over the years.

They parked in front of one of the square brown buildings. All the surrounding buildings had this dusty sheen to them. It reminded Noah of when he shaded his drawings. Yet while he did that on purpose, the dust and grime of these buildings had to be there because no one cared.

Yet the building they were parked in front of was different. It might have been similar in structure to the other buildings, but it was clean. It didn't have that grime. There were no cracked windows or broken light fixtures. No homeless encampments set up near it nor overgrown weeds coming out of cracked sidewalks.

There weren't even signs of it being a school, and no one could be seen, even though they had confirmed an appointment with Mr. Cooper last night. Despite how empty the block seemed and the fact that he didn't see anyone, as Noah glanced up at the tall building, he felt as if he were being watched.

"Are you sure this is the right place?" Mom asked as they got out of the car.

Dad squinted, peering at the address number and his phone. "This is what the GPS says. Maybe we oughta give Mr. Cooper a call to make sure we have the right place."

A young woman stepped out the door of the building. "Forgive me for being late." She had straight, bright red hair and a wide smile on her face. She clapped her hands together. "It's been a busy day." She walked up to Noah's parents and shook their hands. "Mr. and Mrs. Noble, a pleasure to meet you. I'm Jenny, and I shall be your tour guide today." Bending down to Noah, she said, "And this must be Noah. It is an honor." She held out her hand, but Noah didn't take it. Jenny still smiled, not missing a beat. "OK then, shall I show you the tour?"

Mom stared up at the building. "We didn't expect the place to be so...bland."

Jenny laughed putting a hand to her chest. "We're in the process of getting a bigger school. But finding free land is so hard. One day, I envision a great big school with a lawn surrounding it for a mile. And the students can be free to be whatever they want on the campus grounds." Jenny glanced at Noah, a sparkle in her eyes. "But that's years from now. First we must fill this place with students."

Jenny revealed a keycard, unlocking the door with it. As they walked down a long, pristine hallway surrounded by white tiles, the tapping of their shoes reverberated across the floor. At the end of the hallway, next to another door was a man over six feet tall. He wore a black suit with a comical large cap from the thirties. The hat blocked out his features. He didn't say a word but his head turned, following them as they entered and exited the hallway.

"That's security," Jenny said. "We don't have too much trouble over here, but the city being the city, occasionally some vagabond wanders in. They don't stay too long." Jenny held the door open and smiled.

"And I would like to welcome you to the School of Expressive and Extraordinary Young People."

Noah's parents stared at her.

"Sorry," Jenny said, shrugging. "It's a working title."

The long corridor reminded Noah of his own school except that it was bigger. Because of his height, everything seemed bigger. But this was different. These halls reminded him of ones he'd seen on shows and in movies—ones where adults or teenagers go to school. The corridor near the entrance splintered off into different directions.

"Here at the school," Jenny said, "because we have less than a hundred students, Noah would not be placed with other students in his grade like in a public school, but with a group of students around the same age. Because this is a special, more advanced school with smaller classes, there will be more attention given to Noah and the other students to help with their lessons." She stood up straight. "Unlike the overcrowded school system, we give each of our students the attention they need."

"These are the classrooms," Jenny said. "There's about a dozen of them." The hallways curved and Jenny continued. "The cafeteria is right here, and past that is the gym." She turned to Noah and winked. "I think you'll like it. All of our students do."

Dad barked out a laugh. "My son doesn't care for the gym. Maybe when he hits puberty."

"Dad!"

Jenny laughed along with him. "None of them do at first." She led them outside. "This is the courtyard," Jenny said with her arms wide.

The roof had glass panels, letting the sun through. Neat rows of shrubs were situated throughout the courtyard, surrounding the dozens of students there. A cement sidewalk cut through the courtyard, yet most of the students lay on the grass. An older girl had a piercing through her nose. A boy the same age had blue streaks in his hair. The younger kids, those around Noah's age, chased each other around, play-ing games with balls and branches. There weren't any phones or video games or anything else he had gotten

used to. When they stepped outside, all eyes turned to N
oah.

No, not me. My parents. They barely glanced over
Noah. They seemed like regular teenagers, yet there
had to be a reason they were at this school. What
kind of powers did they have and why weren't they on
display?

"This being a weekend," Jenny said. "The students
are free to wear what they want instead of the school
uniform. Now a few of the older students are allowed
out. They've earned it. Despite what the kids think,
this isn't a prison." She and Noah's parents laughed,
but Noah didn't think it was funny. Schools were
prisons in a sense.

A young girl, barely into her teens, rushed up to
them. "Miss Jenny."

"Oh, hello there, Anastasia."

The student introduced herself to them before
sidling up to Jenny. "Do you mind if I come with
you?" she asked her eyes wide. "It's always better to
hear a student's viewpoint."

Jenny smiled. "You're quite right. Come along, dear."

The four of them started to walk but Noah stood still. "Um, I'm sorry, but do you mind if I use the bathroom? It was a long drive over here, and I drank a lot of water."

"Yes, of course."

"Would you like me to show you?" Anastasia asked.

Noah shook his head. "I'm OK. I'll catch up with you. I know where it is. We passed it on the way here."

"OK," Mom said. "Try not to take too long."

"I won't."

Noah left them before they changed their minds, rushing to the bathroom. He just had to get away from it. It all seemed like too much. And what made matters worse was that his parents didn't understand what was going on—what kind of school it was. They thought it was a school for gifted kids. And it was, just not in a way they could have imagined. He had to tell them.

Noah washed his face, staring into the mirror like he had seen his dad do when he was bothered about something. "I don't know what to do," he said, wiping his face.

"Nice hair."

Noah spun around. A much older boy stood behind him, leaning against a stall. He had his arms crossed and he smiled.

"I always wished I could grow a 'fro like that, but my parents wouldn't let me." He shrugged. "Maybe I'll grow it out now? Now there's a thought."

"What do you want?" Noah asked.

"To wash my hands if you'd move to the side." The older boy gestured and Noah stepped aside. "I'd like to be the first to welcome you to SEXY." Once his hands were dry, he held one out. Noah hesitated before shaking his hand.

"SEXY?" Noah's eyes widened, and a smile spread across his face once he realized that was the name of the school.

"Glad to see you're a quick study, mushroom. For all her faults, Jenny is right. They really do need to come up with a new name for this prison." He hopped onto the bathroom counter. "So what's your power?"

"Excuse me?"

"What can you do?" he asked. The tall, lanky kid circled him. "Fly? Move things with your mind? Shoot fire out of your butt? Come on, kid, I'm dying to know."

"I don't even know you."

He narrowed his eyes before relaxing them. "You're right. I've been rude. I'm Jamal." Jamal wore a T-shirt with an eagle logo Noah had never seen before and ripped jeans.

Can I trust him? Noah stared at the boy he had just met. No, he couldn't trust him, but Jeff and Mika had wanted him to spy on the school. Getting to meet the other students here was part of that. And if there were other students like him here, he should be more open about what he could do.

"Noah." He stared into Jamal's dark brown eyes. "And I can disappear."

Jamal gave a soft gasp. "You can fade. We haven't had one of those in a long while."

"What's fade?"

"It's what you can do. Disappearing isn't the right word and neither is vanishing. Fading is…" Jamal cupped his finger to his chin. "Fading is like the world, cameras, people, memory, they all forget about you. You…fade into the background. At least that's what the last fader told us it was like. Does it feel like that?"

Noah nodded. It all made sense. It did feel like that.

"Good. I'm going to give you some advice, mushroom," Jamal said. "Don't trust anyone here, especially Miss Jenny and her flunkies, like Anastasia. They're all looking to get ahead in this prison. Special privileges and such. And believe me, it *is* a prison no matter what they tell you."

There was something about the School of Expressive and Extraordinary Young People that was off. He could hear Mika's voice in his head saying that he should stay to find out more about it. But moving to a new school wasn't what he had in mind. He wanted to go home to his mom's cooking and draw.

A noise rattled in the hallway and Noah turned around, wondering if he had been gone too long.

"Hey, what can you do?" But when Noah looked back, Jamal had left.

Noah left the bathroom, catching up to his parents and Miss Jenny. The three adults stood on a hill in the courtyard. Anastasia was gone and Noah didn't see Jamal anywhere.

"If it isn't our newest student," Jenny said with a wide smile across her face.

Noah narrowed his eyes at her. "What's going on?"

Dad bent down to him. "While you were gone, your mother and I discussed it. Jenny explained everything to us. She explained how this school would hone your art abilities. How they would be able to bring out the best in you, unlike your current school."

"And," Mom said, hugging Noah. "She said they would cover all of your tuition. Isn't that great?"

No, it isn't. "I don't want to go to this school. What about my friends? What about my teachers? What about—"

"Son," Dad said. "It's a great opportunity for you. You'll never get another chance like this."

Noah almost responded but saw Jenny's smiling face. There would be time to convince his parents that this wasn't the right school later. When they were away from prying ears and eyes.

Noah sighed. "OK."

But no matter what Noah said or how hard he tried, he couldn't convince his parents on the ride home. It was like they wouldn't even hear him out, and they always heard him out.

Noah stared through the car window, glimpsing his sad face gazing back at him.

"Don't look so glum, son," Dad said. "I know it's scary at first, but this is a big chance. Besides, it's not like we won't visit you on the holidays. And at least once a month, we'll come up here."

Noah looked at his dad but didn't say anything. He didn't know the real reason Noah was afraid of going to the new school.

"How about we stop and get some ice cream?" Mom said, smiling. "To celebrate."

"That's a good idea, hon."

"Sure," Noah said, shrugging.

The three ended up at a small ice cream and candy shop away from the city. His parents allowed him to get a banana split with three scoops. Normally, Noah would be diving into it, with his parents constantly having to remind him to wipe his face, and he would regret it soon afterward with a terrible bellyache. This time was different. He lifted the spoon, slowly eating a bite. He had eaten it so slowly that it had already begun to melt and his parents had to help him finish it.

"May I be excused?" Noah asked.

"Of course."

As Noah went to the end of the hall to go to the bathroom, he thought of disappearing—no, fading—and running away. But he couldn't do that to his parents. His father had always taught him to face problems head on. *It's how you become a man.*

Noah was so absorbed by his thoughts that when he stepped out of the bathroom, he bumped into someone. "Sorry."

"Noah?"

He looked up and saw his favorite teacher. "Sorry, Ms. Vera. I wasn't paying attention."

"And I thought you were only that way when you were drawing." Ms. Vera smiled, but Noah didn't return it. "Noah, is something wrong?"

Noah bit his lip and looked at the ground. He balled his hands into fists. *Maybe I should tell her. She was always one of the nice ones.*

"I'm going to a new school, Ms. Vera," Noah said. "No matter what I say, my parents are forcing me to go, and I go Monday."

"Oh, I see. What school are you going to?"

"The School of Expressive and Extraordinary Young People."

She cupped her chin. "Hmmm, never heard of it. Come on, let me talk to your parents."

They walked over to them, and Ms. Vera said, "Hi, Mr. and Mrs. Noble. It's a pleasure to see you here."

"We thought it'd be nice to treat Noah," Dad said. "He got accepted to a new school."

"So I heard. I've never heard of it, and I try to keep up on these kinds of things. Can you tell me a bit about it?"

"Sure," Mom said, nodding. "We only just learned of it ourselves, but Jenny was very helpful."

Ms. Vera sat down and his parents told her about the school they had just gone to. Normally, having a teacher talk to his parents would have made Noah nervous, even if he hadn't done anything wrong. Noah didn't feel that way now. He hoped that Ms. Vera could change his parents' minds. He needed an ally that wasn't a kid. Adults never listened to kids, but they always listened to other adults.

Ms. Vera dropped the spoon in her sundae and leaned forward when Noah's parents were finished. "Mr. and Mrs. Noble, don't you think all of this is a bit sudden?"

"We thought so too," Dad said, shaking his head. "But it's still early enough in the year for Noah not to fall too far behind. And they want him enrolled as soon as possible. They say he shows great promise."

Noah's parents smiled with pride, and the heat on Noah's neck rose. Aside from disappearing, or fading, there was nothing special about him.

Ms. Vera gently set her hand on his mom's arm. "Mrs. Noble, Emma, I love your son. I normally don't say this until after they graduate, but he's one of my favorite students."

"I am?"

She nodded. "Uh-huh. Now, I shouldn't be saying this, but as much as I like him and have enjoyed him in my class, he's...he's not the best student. His grades have been average at best, but he does try his hardest and is a positive force in the classroom."

Mom's eyes turned to Noah, and he slunk deeper into the booth. *Maybe she can't do anything for me.*

"We know that," Mom said. "But the school doesn't want him for his grades."

"That's right!" Noah said. "They want me for my abilities!"

Ms. Vera's normally kind blue eyes hardened as they stared at him. "Is that so?"

"Yes," Noah shrieked. He glanced at the table, wanting to say more. But as nice as Ms. Vera was, she wouldn't believe him either. None of the adults would.

Dad nodded, sipping a cup of coffee. "As much as we've told Noah about his grades, we know that."

"Sorry," Noah said, shrugging.

"Yes," Mom said, "the woman there, Jenny, said they wanted him for his art. It's a school for creative people, not academics."

"And I told you the boy's art would be good for something," Dad said, smiling. "I don't know where he gets it from. Neither of us is good at drawing."

"Oh, look at the time," Mom said, glancing down at her watch. "We really must be going. Noah has to pack for his new school."

"Yes, of course," Ms. Vera said, rising. "It was great having you in my class, Noah. I'm going to miss you around school."

Noah sighed, realizing that as much as he liked her, not even she could help him. He was on his own. "I'm going to miss you too, Ms. Vera." Noah hugged her legs, squeezing tightly.

Ms. Vera bent down and returned the hug, stroking his afro. Normally, he hated it but right now he didn't mind.

"I'm going to miss you too," she said. "I hope I'll see you again during winter break." Ms. Vera sadly smiled. "I wish I had one of your drawings to hang in my classroom."

"We'll try to get you one," Dad said. "He has so many."

"It better be a good one," Noah said.

Ms. Vera smiled. "Then you pick it, Noah."

"I will."

Ms. Vera reached into her purse, digging out an old receipt. She wrote on it before handing it to him. "Here's my number and address if you need to reach me. Good bye, Noah. I'm glad you were in my class and I got to know you."

As Ms. Vera walked away, Noah couldn't help but wonder if that was the last time he'd ever see her.

"That was nice of her," Mom said.

"Come on, son," Dad said. "We got a lot of packing to do."

"I hope there's a teacher like that in your new school," Mom said. "It's so hard to find a good teacher."

"Yeah, it is," Noah said, watching his favorite teacher disappear

***

"This is a great opportunity!" Mika said, smiling. The three of them were huddled in their secret hiding place.

Noah shook his head. "I don't think you get that I'm not going to see you for a while. And who knows what they're going to do to me while I'm in there."

"Oh, we get it," Jeff said with a mouthful of cookies. Wiping his mouth on his sleeve, he said, "We just think it's a great chance for us too. Come on, buddy, you got to look at it this way. You're going into a secret school where you get to meet other kids with powers. It's like a comic book."

Noah couldn't help but smile, remembering all the comic books they'd read and movies they'd watched over the years. "You make it sound exciting."

"It can be. Think of it like you're a spy or something."

"But I'll be all alone in a strange place. I won't have you guys."

"I'm going to work on that," Mika said. She pushed up her glasses on her nose.

"What? You going to hack into their system?" Jeff asked.

"Maybe one day, but no. We may not be able to get inside, but at least we know where it is. That's one more thing we didn't know yesterday."

"But—"

"I know you're nervous and scared, Noah," Mika said. "Even though we won't be with you physically, we'll always be here for you."

Jeff grinned. "Yeah, buddy. Like always. Nothing's changed."

Mika moved in to hug Noah. "Thanks." Jeff wiped his hands and did the same. The three of them embraced, smothering the smaller Noah, but he didn't mind. They were his friends.

"What kind of pizza is your mom getting?" Jeff asked.

"Oh God," Mika said, rolling her eyes. "Why are you always thinking about food?"

"Because I'm hungry."

"Whatever kind of pizza you want since it's my last night here," Noah said. "We can even get our own."

CHAPTER 13

NOAH STARED UP at the large vacant building. He had said goodbye to his parents moments ago. They'd promised to write and call. As he glanced up at Miss Jenny's back, he wasn't sure if they would allow him such luxuries at this school. He still couldn't believe they'd sent him away no matter how much he had pleaded and begged.

Miss Jenny turned to look back down at him, hugging a tablet against her chest. "I know you're scared, Noah, but you're going to love it here. I couldn't tell your parents this, but this school is the best place for you to learn your powers. There are very few places like this in the world." Miss Jenny scrunched up her face and tapped her lip. "Although with people like us popping up all over, there's bound to be more. Are you ready?"

No. But Noah nodded his head.

Jenny led them through the entrance again. Noah struggled to keep up not only because of his short stature and her long legs, but because he had both a backpack and a suitcase in tow.

"Class is going to start shortly," she said, "but first I have to take you to the doctor's office and then your room. They know you'll be a little late. Most new students are."

When they arrived at the doctor's office, sweat dripped down Noah's back. He plopped on the seat near the door and dropped his backpack.

An older woman with her dark gray hair in a bun stood in the small room. She narrowed her beady eyes at them. "You're late."

"Mrs. Crenshaw, please," Jenny said. "You know how first days go."

Mrs. Crenshaw snorted. "Uh-huh." She looked at her digital pad. "Noah Nobles, please sit on the bed."

Noah did as she asked, thankful that Miss Jenny was in the room. He shivered when Mrs. Crenshaw's gloved hand touched him on the back of his neck.

"Now, Noah," Jenny said, "this is a shot for the school. It's so the other students won't get sick. You understand."

He nodded. "I've had shots before. I'm immune."

She smiled. "You mean you've had your vaccinations. This is a bit different, I'm afraid, because of our...unique physiology. Don't worry. Everyone has had them. I promise it won't hurt."

"Such unruly hair," Mrs. Crenshaw said, bending Noah's neck down.

"Ow." A sharp prick struck the back of his neck.

"There. All done."

"Come on," Jenny said. "Let's get you settled in and then head to class."

Noah rubbed his neck on the way out. He didn't like the way Mrs. Crenshaw's eyes followed him as they left.

Jenny led Noah to the dormitory. The room was so large, and there were neatly made beds everywhere.

No students were in sight. Jenny led him to one of the beds. In front of it was an open, empty chest, and on the bed was a uniform.

"Put your things in the chest," Jenny said. "Get dressed as fast as you can. There'll be time to get you settled in and your belongings put away later. You mustn't be too late for class."

"OK," Noah said as she left. He held up the white dress shirt and khaki shorts along with the dark blue blazer. "What have I gotten into?"

"Perfect," Miss Jenny said, smiling. "But we must make you presentable." She adjusted Noah's collar and flattened out his shirt as he did his best not to squirm. "Better." She reached out then stopped. "Are you sure you don't want to do something about your hair?"

Noah frowned. "No."

"I had to ask." She scrunched her eyes. "You'll need to wear a tie."

"But I don't know how to do it."

"Neither do I. Lucky for us, it's your first day and they won't mind too much. At least, I hope not."

"What—"

"There'll be plenty of time for questions later," she said. "But first we must get you settled. Come along now."

Noah rolled up his sleeves as he went. He was thankful that Jeff didn't see him in this outfit. He would have thought it ridiculous.

Jeff. Mika. Noah missed his friends. He missed his comfortable, crowded halls. He missed how he knew that the water fountain by the science room only shot out clean water for three seconds before squirting brown. He missed that overhead light in the bathroom that always flickered at noon. He missed Ms. Vera's warming smile and Mr. Hill's lack of one. *How could my parents leave me here?*

The halls of this new school were too loud. The shoes they'd given him squeaked with each step he took. And the halls of the school were oddly empty. Miss Jenny said it was because everyone was in class, but at Noah's old school, there would be stragglers, hall monitors, janitors, and random visitors. This place felt so empty.

"Here we are," Jenny said, smiling and placing her hand on the door knob. "Would you like to go in first?"

"No…I'm OK."

She bent down and pinched his cheek. "Don't be nervous, Noah. You'll do great. Remember what you're here for."

Noah took a deep breath. He did. He wasn't here for Miss Jenny or Mr. Cooper. He was here for his friends, Jeff and Mika, and to learn more about this school.

"OK," he said.

Miss Jenny opened the door and walked into the room. It was a small classroom with not more than a dozen students. They weren't all Noah's age. Some of them were either a few years older or a few years younger. All of the students looked at Noah with intense eyes.

"Miss Dawson," Jenny said, "I have your newest student, Noah Noble. I hope you'll forgive his tardiness."

Miss Dawson had short black hair with bright blue eyes. She stopped working on the large screen in front of the classroom and walked over to them.

Holding out her hand, Miss Dawson smiled. "Hello, Noah. Nice to meet you. Welcome to my classroom. Thanks for bringing him, Jenny."

"Good luck, Noah," Jenny said. "I promise I'll come check in with you later to see how you're doing. Goodbye, class!"

Most of the students mumbled goodbye as Miss Jenny walked out the door. Noah glanced at the door. He might not have trusted or even known Miss Jenny, but she was the only thing familiar to him at his new school.

"Noah, please take a seat," Miss Dawson said. She motioned at an empty desk with a tablet on it. "I'm going to guide the other students in what to do and then I'll be over to you. If you wake up the tablet, there's an introduction guide to the school and what we expect from you. Understand?"

"Yes, ma'am."

Miss Dawson smiled. "Good."

Noah walked to his seat and did his best to smile. "Hi," he eked out to another student near his age, tasting how dry his mouth was. She turned away from him in her seat and when Noah looked at the other students near him, they did the same.

Noah frowned and sat down. It was like the first day of school all over again, except there were no friendly faces or people he knew. Even when he had changed schools, there had always been one person he knew. Here, he knew no one. He was all alone.

Noah opened the tablet and read the guide, doing his best to focus his mind on school for once. It was just like any other syllabus except it was electronic. Tablets and computers were familiar to Noah, but the schools he'd been to didn't have electronics that were as new and clean as those at SEXY; they'd been old hand-me-downs. And there weren't enough of even those to go around. As Noah read the syllabus, it didn't mention anything about the students or their powers. Wasn't that the whole point of the school?

There it is.

There was one sentence that mentioned it.

Students are not to use their abilities unless instructed to. Failure to abide by this rule will result in harsh consequences.

Harsh consequences? *What does that mean?*

"Sorry, I took so long," Miss Dawson said, coming over to him. "Did you read everything?"

Noah nodded. "As much as I could."

"It's all right. This is a different school from what you're used to."

He nodded. "It is. I'm not used to all the tech. We used old dusty books most of the time."

She chuckled. "We here at the School of Expressive and Extraordinary Young People try to have all the latest technology to help you students learn. We teach a little differently than what you're used to. What you've experienced over the years is not the most effective way. We make mistakes, but we're able to change the curriculum if we need to. We're looking to the future, Noah. And you students are that future."

Noah didn't understand what she meant by that, but he nodded. Adults always loved it when kids nodded and smiled as if they understood a word of what they had just said.

Miss Dawson smiled. "Good. There's an app specifically designed for you and your grade level. We also incorporated things you learned from your former school. I'm going to be around to help you and guide you if you have any questions. There are a few kids around your age here," she said, placing a hand on a boy's shoulder.

"This is Devin. Devin, I need you to help our newest student here."

"Yes, ma'am."

"Good boy," she said. "Noah, you will work with Devin and other students here for group projects. We believe that students should learn from each other, not just from teachers or dusty books." She grinned. "I'll be back to check on you in a little while."

"OK."

Noah opened the app and began reading the lesson. As his eyes wandered over the words and he answered the questions and did the tests that popped up every now and then, he yawned. This wasn't what he had been expecting. Both Mr. Cooper and Miss Jenny had said that he was at this school to learn more about his abilities. And here he was doing boring school work. He could have stayed in Mr. Hill's class for that. Although the apps he used were far more interesting than any of Mr. Hill's boring lectures, Noah had a hard time concentrating.

He spotted an app for note taking and opened it. Noah grinned. The school, teachers, and approach to learning might be different, but some things never changed.

Noah took the stylus, adjusting his small hands to how big and awkward it was. But soon the fear and the awkwardness of the new school faded. All that mattered to him was the screen and his imagination.

As soon as Noah became lost in thought, a sharp pain struck the back of his neck. He screamed.

Miss Dawson rushed over to him. "Noah!" She helped him sit up. "Are you all right?"

"I'm OK." *What was that?* The pain that had attacked him a second ago had vanished. He rubbed his neck, trying to figure out what had caused it.

"Noah," she said in a soft voice. "You shouldn't try to access your powers when you're not told to. You'll get hurt."

All the kids in the class looked at him not as the strange new student, but with sympathy in their eyes.

"I want you to go to the doctor's office and have Mrs. Crenshaw check you out."

Noah shivered, remembering the cold look in the doctor's eyes. He didn't want to go there if he didn't have to.

Ding. Ding. Ding.

The noise may have been different, but the result was still the same. All the kids rushed out of class. Noah slid out of his desk to do the same.

"Noah, please see Mrs. Crenshaw."

"OK, I will!" Noah said, blending in with the rest of the hurrying kids. "If I have time."

Noah continued rubbing his neck as he followed the throng of kids down the hallway. The kids made their way to the courtyard. Noah would rather have stayed in the classroom and draw. Maybe there was a corner where he could be left alone.

"Tried to use your powers," a voice said, hiding between the lockers.

Noah jumped but relaxed when he saw Jamal. Noah lifted his hand to soothe the back of his neck but stopped when he saw Jamal's eyes.

"The doctor...," Noah said.

Jamal smiled and rubbed Noah's afro. Noah slapped his hand away. "Smart, and spunky. I like that, mushroom. You didn't really believe that it was some sort of vaccine shot, did you?"

"No," Noah said, glancing down at his feet. *How could I be so stupid? Of course it wasn't a vaccine.* Mika would be very disappointed in him. She'd told him not to trust the school while he was there.

"Uh-huh. So how do you like our school? I told you you'd wind up here."

Noah perked up. *That's right. He did tell me that.* "How did you know?"

"Never trust any of the adults around here," Jamal said. "Especially Jenny. She was one of us, you know. But the school corrupted her. She can make those not like us very agreeable. Like parents."

"Leave the new kid alone," a teenaged girl said. Her dark green eyes glared at Jamal, peeking out from the dark makeup on her face. Purple streaks ran through her black hair and long sleeves covered part of her hands. "Don't you have anything better to do?"

Jamal rolled his eyes. "God, Elise, don't *you* have anything better to do? Unlike you, I'm helping out the new kid for once."

She stepped between them. "I bet. Come on, I'll be the one who will show you around." Elise put her arm around Noah and led him down the hall to the courtyard.

"What's your name?" she asked.

"Noah."

"Nice name." She reached out toward his head but then stopped. "May I?"

Noah normally hated it when people touched his hair, but she was kind enough to ask.

"OK," he said.

"Soft."

He looked up and smiled. "Thank you."

Elise returned his smile. "Listen, I'm going to give it to you straight. School here is pretty chill, at least compared to where I was before. They're not much of a grading type. I swear, we could all get Fs and they'd still not do anything. They want us for our powers and what we can do for them."

"And what can we do for them?"

Elise sighed. "I wish I knew, Noah. I wish I knew. I haven't figured that out yet."

Ding. Ding. Ding.

"Come on, let me walk you back to your class," she said. "Listen, if there's anything you need let me know. I know what it was like to be the new kid."

Noah nodded. He had already thanked her and said goodbye when he realized that he didn't even know what either Elise or Jamal could do.

CHAPTER 14

*D*ING. DING.

Noah looked up from his assignment. *Two bells?* All the students quickly got up from their desks, nearly sprinting from the classroom.

"What's going on?" Noah asked Devin.

"Gym time," he said with a smile on his face. "Get dressed."

Noah rushed back to his dorm room to change. He wore shorts and a white T-shirt with the school's logo, which looked like a model of an atom emblazoned on it, along with the name of the school. As much as he hurried, by the time he got to the gym, he was the last one there, swallowing deep breaths.

The kids were in groups, milling around, but not grouped by age as they had been at lunch or during recess. Kids of different ages were together, the older kids weren't annoyed by the younger kids. They were even friendly and talking with them.

As Noah scanned the room, he didn't see anything he associated with gym. There were no jump ropes or tetherballs. No basketballs or tennis balls. None of the normal equipment he had seen over the years. There were a few large blue mats scattered about and that was it.

Noah took a step but then realized he didn't know where to go. He was the new kid, and he was far too small for any of the sports they were about to do just like all the other times in gym. Basketball, baseball, soccer, volleyball, it didn't matter. He was always picked last and no one wanted him on their team. A lot of the kids in the gym stopped their conversations and turned their eyes toward him. Noah squirmed. *It's going to be a long class.*

"Welcome to the fun part of SEXY," Jamal said from behind. He clapped Noah's back so hard he nearly knocked him down. "If ninety percent of the school was like this, it might not be such a bad place."

"I've never been much for gym," Noah said. "I'm small."

"This isn't that type of gym. This is the place where we practice our powers. It's why we're here. They might call it a gym, but it's more of a training ground."

Noah couldn't help but smile. *This is why I'm here.* And he would finally see what other kids' powers were. No wonder the other kids stared at him. They wanted to see what Noah was capable of. Noah was about to ask Jamal what he could do when his eyes came upon the man who guarded the entrance. The man stood as still as a statue, never moving except for his eyes. And even when he blinked there was something off about them.

The timing is always the same.

The man's skin looked clammy and pale but without the sweat. Noah stared at his ears, which were perfect. In fact, everything about him was perfect. Not one body part was longer than the other, and there wasn't a blemish anywhere on him.

The man turned his blank expression on Noah, chilling him.

Jamal grabbed Noah by the collar. "Stay away from those things."

"What is he?" Noah asked, turning back to look at him. "And why's he staring at me?"

"He?" Jamal asked. "No, no, no. That *thing* isn't a person. It's a kind of advanced robot."

Noah watched the machine as it stared at the kids in the gym, cocking its head from side to side. That would explain why its features were bland and why it didn't quite look human.

"I thought I told you to leave him alone," Elise said.

"God," Jamal said, rolling his eyes. "Didn't realize you were a narc. I was just telling Noah about our jailers, a fact you didn't think he should know."

Elise turned to look at the robot and scratched her arm through her long-sleeved shirt. "Jamal's right...for once. Stay away from those machines."

"I don't get it," Noah said. "What can they do?"

"They're the school's attack dogs," Jamal said. "As far as I know, there's three of them on campus. One at the entrance, one here, and one patrolling the grounds." He shrugged. "Could be more for all I know. They seem docile, but don't let that fool you. Years ago, a student escaped from here—from them."

Elise rolled her eyes. "Pssh. That's just a rumor."

"Suit yourself."

A man in his late twenties came up to the three. His suit jacket hung over his shoulder and his white shirt collar was undone. "Noah! A pleasure to meet you." He smiled. "Call me, Sam. I'm in charge of the school. Sort of like its principal." He patted Noah on the back and Noah nearly fell over. "Glad to see you're getting to know some of our other students here."

"Oh yeah," Jamal said with a smirk. "We're the best role models the school has. Perfect for the new kid here."

"Right," Sam said. "I appreciate it. Noah, why don't you come with me? Unfortunately, you're not in the same class as Jamal. However, you are in the same class as Elise."

Sam led Noah to the other side of the gym. "This gym is where you'll be trained to use your powers." He crouched down and pointed to the other groups of kids. "All the kids here are grouped together according to their powers and there's a teacher assigned to each of them."

"You mean there are kids with the same powers?" Noah asked, wondering if there was another kid like him.

Sam chuckled. "No, no. I mean there are kids with more...how can I put it, aggressive powers, and kids like you. Kids whose powers aren't quite as aggressive or flashy. We try to group them accordingly, but since we're still new at this, kids can be moved around." Sam smiled. "Come now. Noah, I'd like you to meet Mrs. Carter."

Mrs. Carter came over, her hand touching her short, straight hair. "Oh my. That's quite a head of hair you have."

Noah frowned.

She straightened her skirt. "I hear you're already advanced for someone your age. That's good. Real good. Gym is about to start. Let's get you ready."

"Goodbye, Noah," Sam said. "And good luck."

Noah found himself in a group of about a dozen students. He made his way to the only person he knew, Elise. "Hi," he said.

"I knew you'd find your way back to me," she said with a smirk on her face.

"Attention, class," Mrs. Carter said. "We have a new student with us, Noah. Please say hello to him."

"Hello, Noah," the class said in a half-hearted way. Elise nudged Noah and gave him a smile.

"All we ask is that you improve with each session," Mrs. Carter said. "In whatever way possible. We will help you in any way we can." She stared at one of the younger kids. "Riley, are you ready?"

A kid smaller than Noah with disheveled hair hesitated before nodding. Unlike all the other kids in the gym, he sighed and frowned. *He's not excited to be here.*

Ring. Ring. Riiing!

All the kids in the gym except for Noah and Riley yelled out in joy.

A loud crackling noise caused Noah to flinch. He spun around, watching a teenaged girl laugh as bright sparks danced on her fingers. A tall boy melted into the floor. It was as if his insides became water.

Gross.

A boy and a girl crossed arms before standing with their backs together. They turned around, grinning, and clapped their hands together. A bright, blinding light enveloped them. When Noah's eyes came to, they were gone, replaced by a tall being of pure light.

He, she, no they, shone like the sun, their bright light blinding everyone in the gym.

"Turn it down, you two!" Sam said.

Their color dimmed into a dark blue.

A boy leapt into the air and hopped onto their head. He smiled before leaping off. The being of light flashed colors, chasing the boy.

Noah grinned. He reminded him of a frog. "Wow."

"Wow, indeed," Mrs. Carter said. "Now, Noah, I understand this is your first day, but we need to see with our own eyes how advanced you are and point out any strengths or weaknesses you may have so that you may better control your powers. Understand?"

"Yes, ma'am." He paused. "What do I do?"

"What you were born to do, dear."

"Mrs. Carter," Elise said, stepping forward. "Do you mind if I help him out?"

She nodded. "Of course. That's why we're all here." Mrs. Carter walked away.

"Touch my hand." Elise extended her hand to Noah, but he hesitated. "You don't need to be afraid."

Noah puffed his chest out. "I'm not. What...can you do?"

"Trust me?"

Noah took a deep breath. "All right."

Noah tensed as he grabbed her hand, expecting a jolt or for his hand to disappear. He had no idea what the other students in the school could do. Instead, what he saw was Elise. Her heavy makeup receded and her black hair faded into a lush blond.

"Wow," Noah said. "You're beautiful."

Elise blushed. "Thank you."

Noah turned to find what else he could see when a dark ten-foot monster turned its red eyes to him. It snarled and he yelled, letting go of Elise's hand and fumbling until he stumbled and hit the ground. The monster vanished and, in its place, Noah found the sentry staring directly at him.

"Sorry about that," Elise said.

"What was that?"

"I have the ability to create illusions when I'm touching someone," she said. "They can see what I want."

"Oh. So is that how you really look beneath all the dark makeup?"

She raised an eyebrow and shrugged. "Anyway, I'd forgotten how I imagine the sentries."

"As monsters."

Elise nodded. "As monsters."

"Why?"

"Jamal isn't always full of shit. Things aren't what they appear to be. And while a sentry is watching us to make sure we don't escape, it particularly focuses on our little group."

"How come?"

Elise leaned in and whispered. "Because we're the most dangerous."

A kid flicked a lighter and a huge ball of flame exploded from her hand. She grinned as it rose and grew into a large bird and dove past a student. She cackled in delight as the flames blossomed around her.

"Ada!" a teacher shouted at her. "Control your flame!"

A cloud of mist hovered down from above and smothered Ada's fire. The mist pulled together until it became a human shape. The girl who was once mist smiled. "Yeah, control your flame."

Ada screamed and blossomed a fireball in her hand. The other girl faded into mist and floated away with Ada chasing her.

A kid rolled into a ball and bounced around the gym. He smiled and laughed as he careened off the walls and even smashed into the other students. He headed for a wall, when a shadow tore itself from the wall and grabbed him.

We're the most dangerous ones? Noah thought. But then he realized that the entire school was dangerous in their own way, and he remembered the school shooter.

Noah caught Mrs. Carter looking at him, and he remembered to use his powers. He took a deep breath, letting the excitement of his first day drain out of him. He ignored all the surrounding laughter and yelling until he faded from this world.

Can I leave? But as soon as Noah faded, the sentry turned its watchful gaze on him, its red eyes glowing. No matter what move he made or what the kids around him did, it watched him. Thankfully, it didn't seem to be making any move against him. *What can it do?*

Neither the teachers nor the sentry seemed to be pushing Noah to do anything. It was a gym with mats, balls, and cones, but the students either ignored them or used them for their own purposes. One girl hovered three balls in the air. Another student's long hair melted into different colors. He whipped his hair forward and coated it with paint, making funny faces in it.

It was a lot to take in even for Noah. He and his friends had discussed this before, but there was a difference between discussing it and witnessing it. And all Noah could do was disappear from the world. Not a very useful superpower. He didn't understand Elise's saying they were the most dangerous.

Noah spotted Jamal and wondered what he could do. Now that no one except the sentry could see Noah, he could finally learn what kind of powers the older kid had. He just had to make his way through the throngs of taller students.

Noah craned his neck as he walked around the gym, inching his way around the students and dodging them and their strange abilities.. He tried not to stare at the sentry that was staring at him. On the mat not ten feet from him was the younger, smaller boy, Riley. He sat cross-legged, closing his eyes so hard that veins ran across his forehead. Riley's teeth were clenched and beads of sweat dripped down his face.

What can he do?

"Go away!" Riley shouted.

Noah stopped. Could Riley see something terrifying or something inside people? Was that why he closed his eyes? Noah tiptoed around him, but Riley turned his neck and stared at him.

"Go away!"

"You can see me?" Noah asked.

But Riley didn't answer. He didn't stare at Noah but through him.

"Just go away," Riley said, rocking back and forth and hugging himself into a ball.

Noah bent down and stopped using his powers. He slowly reached out to Riley. "Are you all right?"

As soon as Noah touched him, Riley let out a loud scream.

All the students in the gym stopped and stared at Noah.

Ding.

"All right, everybody," Mrs. Carter said. "Gym's up. Get cleaned up, especially you two," she said, eyeing the paint that was all over two girls in the corner. "Time for lunch."

All the students' powers had disappeared, and they headed out of the gym. Noah turned to apologize to Riley but he was gone.

CHAPTER 15

ALL THE STUDENTS might have had had similar interests, but it was still a new school with old rules. And Noah found himself eating alone in the cafeteria. He had thought that perhaps Elise or Jamal eat with him, but he realized it was stupid. Whatever groups and pairings the students might have had in gym, based on their powers, were no longer necessary. Noah had thought that a fresh, hot meal in the cafeteria might ease the pain of being alone. But it only made him miss his mother's tightly packed and organized lunches in little bags and boxes.

Noah pulled out his notebook. Being alone was something he was used to. It was why he'd taken to drawing. If he couldn't have his friends or mom's lunches, he might as well do something that was very familiar to him.

Noah readied himself to draw. But when he looked up, a young face stared back at him.

"Why did you approach me?" Riley asked. "No one approaches me."

Noah scratched his cheek, unsure of what to do. He shrugged. "I don't know. You seemed like you needed help."

Riley bowed his head. "Sorry. I'm just not used to people trying to help me anymore." He sighed. "I can sense people's intentions with my powers."

"Ooh. You're a mind reader."

Riley shook his head. "No. An...empath, Mrs. Carter said. Or empath-like. I can read people's feelings. It's a bit much."

"That's how you knew I was there."

"Yeah, but you're not like the others," Riley said, squirming in his seat. "You didn't feel disgusted by me."

"Should I have?" Noah asked.

"Guess not. But it's not because you're new that you didn't feel like the others do. You're different."

"I don't know about that, but you reminded me of me when I first had my powers. I thought I could help. We're all in this together, right? At least that's what I've been told."

Riley rolled his eyes. "You're not going to tell me I need to concentrate and breathe and focus my chi or whatever, are you? That's the stuff the adults say around here and it's not working."

Noah shook his head. "No, I—"

"Hi, Noah," Elise said, coming from behind and ruffling his hair. "You did great today. Hi, Riley."

"Hello," he said with no emotion on his face.

"I'm glad you're here, Noah," she said. "I'll see you around." A passing glance took place between Riley and Elise.

"What's going on with you guys? Elise is friendly."

"I agree. She was once friendly to me. But things have been different since I started using my powers." Riley looked over his shoulder. "She's friendly, but very fearful. She carries with her a great pain."

"Really? Do you know why?"

"Uh-uh," Riley said. "They say with time and patience, I can learn...like become, like, a really good therapist or something. But first I need to control my powers."

"I may have an idea," Noah said.

During recess, Noah and Riley sat across from each other on a small grassy hill.

Riley shielded his eyes from the sun. "Are you sure about this?"

"No, but I wanted to try something new." Noah shrugged. "It's just an idea. We don't have to do it."

Riley paused. "No, we can try it." He ripped out a tuft of grass and blew it from his hand. "There's not much else to do around here."

"What do you like to do? For fun?"

"Play video games. But they don't have that around here. They say it's a waste of our gifts or something.

I haven't touched a video game since I got here. It's maddening."

"Anything else you like to do, like a hobby or something besides video games?"

Riley shrugged. "I love gaming."

Noah leaned over, placing his head on his hand. *This is going to be harder than I thought.*

"Well, there is something else. I used to play board games with my mom and uncle." Riley smiled for the first time since Noah met him. "Every Friday night, we'd have a board game night. I'd stay up for hours. I miss those." Riley sighed. "All they have here are those really old games like Monopoly and Risk. My mom and uncle hated those games growing up. Took forever and people never played by the right rules."

Noah perked up. An idea was forming in his head. "You wanna teach me those games sometime? I've never played."

Suspicion formed in Riley's stern eyes. "Never? OK. I'm not sure if you'll like it. We can meet after you get oriented. Miss Jenny will come to show you around and tell you what chores you are to do and how to keep your bed." Riley leaned in closer. "They like it nice and neat around here."

Noah nodded. "But after, you can play board games with me?"

"Sure. We have a lot of free time around here once we get the chores and homework done."

As soon as classes were over, Miss Jenny found Noah and asked him how his day went. She showed what he would be responsible for, like taking out the trash and washing the dishes. Every student had their own chores. She showed him what they expected when it came to clean uniforms and a tidy bed. Miss Jenny was also delighted that he had made friends with Riley. Since they were the same age, Riley's bed was right next to Noah's.

Riley came after he was done with his chores and Miss Jenny had left. Riley taught Noah the game. Other students kept walking by and eyeing the boys while they were playing. But as time passed, they never once stopped and joined in.

"Don't worry about it," Riley said, looking up as he finished moving his piece. "You'll learn in this school your powers can also separate you from people."

The bell chime rang and Riley looked up. He sighed, looking at the pile of money and property on his side. "You picked up the game fast."

"Thanks for teaching me the game. I liked it."

"Yeah, well, I'm glad you enjoyed it," Riley said. "But trust me, there's far better games out there. I think I can convince them to buy one. But we'd have to have at least another player. A lot of the games don't work with two."

"Look who has a new friend," Jamal said, walking up from behind and clapping Noah on the back. "You sure do like making friends with all the outcasts, mushroom."

"Hey, they're not outcasts," Noah said. "And I'd wish you'd stop calling me that."

"Relax. I'm only kidding. Monopoly, huh? Haven't played that one since I was a little kid."

"You could always play with us."

Jamal eyed Riley, but Riley never once looked at Jamal. "Nah, I think I'll pass. I'm too old for kiddie games. See you around...mushroom."

Riley finally looked up when Jamal was gone. "You need to be more careful with the friends you make at this school."

"Why? Jamal was the first person I met during orientation. He's a pain, but he's OK, I guess."

"He was? He didn't talk to me until two weeks later, and it wasn't anything kind." Riley glanced in the direction Jamal had gone. "There's something about him. During gym, I used to be able to feel his anger. Now I don't feel anything at all. It's as if he walled himself off from me. He's dangerous."

"What's his power? What can he do?"

"Hey new kid," a young boy said, stopping in front of them. "You wanna get ready for bed. It's going to be lights out. They won't be as harsh on you because you're new, but that won't last long. Riley will show you what to do." The kid went to the empty bed next to Noah's and lay down.

Noah and Riley cleaned up and put away the game, and Riley showed Noah what he had to do to get ready for bed. While they were in their respective beds, Riley said to Noah, "Psst. I thought you were going to show me a way to control my powers. All we did was play games."

"I promise. I will."

Riley frowned before rolling over to his side.

Noah stared up at the ceiling, doing his best to ignore all the sounds in the dorm. The older kids were still allowed up. Even though they spoke in hushed tones, Noah heard their murmurings. He had been to sleepovers before and had hosted them. Well, it was really with just Jeff and that new kid who moved away as quickly as he came. He sighed. This was different. He missed his room. He missed his mom and dad. He missed his friends.

Noah rolled over and hugged the blankets closer to him, the school shooting replaying in his mind. He whispered, "I have to remember why I'm doing this."

CHAPTER 16

THE NEXT DAY, Noah found himself in the gym again. He stood next to Riley as they still had a few minutes before gym started.

Riley fidgeted, staring up at the clock. "You shouldn't be next to me. I can't stand it when people are next to me. The closer someone is to me, the more I feel their emotions. But the teachers—or those things—won't let me leave the gym. They say it's good for me. That I have to learn to get past it. That I'm young." Riley shook his head and sighed. "But they don't understand."

Noah sat down next to him. "No, they don't."

"What are you doing? I just said—"

"I know what you said." Noah softened his tone. "I just wanted to talk about yesterday's game. We have a few minutes 'till the bell rings anyway. After that, I'll leave you alone."

Riley narrowed his eyes then nodded. "OK."

"How did you know what properties to buy?" Noah asked. "I was trying to save my money for the more expensive ones. They give more money if you land on it."

"Yeah, but they're also more expensive to buy. If you can only buy one or two of the expensive ones, I may land on them and pay you. But if you buy more of the cheaper ones, odds are you'll land on my properties more than I'll land on yours. As my uncle used to say, 'Easy money.'" Riley gave him a small smile.

"Wow. Never thought of it like that, but it makes sense. How'd you come upon that strategy?"

"My uncle and mom taught me. It wasn't until they'd beat me countless times that my mom finally told me, and I got it. She said that I needed to look at things differently and see not just what I wanted to do but what would happen because of it." Riley shrugged. "Ever since then, I apply that to all the games I play. Or try to." Riley glanced up at the clock. "Hey, you should—"

"What other kinds of games do you play that you think I might like?" Noah asked. "The ones you and your mom and uncle used to play?"

Riley's eyes went wide. "Oh man, there's a whole bunch." He paused. "My mom always thought there was a couple of—she called them gateway games—that people should try first. Like King of Tokyo. I think I mentioned that before. And, I didn't realize there were games where you could work together. Pandemic was another good one."

Ding. Ding. Ding.

Riley cried out and put his hands to his head.

"Hey," Noah said. "Hey! Tell me about Pandemic. What's it about and how do you win?"

Mrs. Carter walked next to them. She eyed them before walking away.

"It's..." Riley rocked his head. "It's..."

"It's what? What's it about?"

Riley gritted his teeth together. "It's a game where you try to save the world from viruses. You travel around the world and try to match cards to eliminate the different color viruses. You—"

A girl flew by overhead and Riley ducked his head.

"Riley," Noah said, shouting over the commotion of the other kids. "How do you win?"

Riley opened his eyes, staring directly at Noah. He stopped fidgeting and there was a calm in his eyes as he spoke.

Noah didn't exactly understand what Riley said about the board game or its strategies. But he didn't need to. Noah had wanted Riley to talk about something he was passionate about so that all the emotions he felt due to his power would be nothing but background noise to him.

He listened to Riley for the entire session. None of the teachers, sentries, or other students came to bother him despite the fact that he didn't even bother to use his powers himself. Noah thought that they might come, but they never did.

The bell chimed. Riley stopped talking and looked up. "Oh, it's over. That was quick. Not like before."

"How do you feel?"

"Good. All the emotions didn't overwhelm me. Thank you." Riley paused then stared at him. "How did you know to do that?"

Noah shrugged. "It was a guess, really. I think people have their own ways of controlling their powers. When I was first using mine, I didn't know it at the time, but I would fade when I was doing something I loved—drawing. I thought maybe you'd be like me. If you took your mind off things and thought about what you enjoyed, then maybe it wouldn't hurt so bad."

"Oh." Riley scratched his head. "No one's really explained it to me. It helped."

"Riley and Noah," Mrs. Carter said. "Class is over. Go get yourselves cleaned up then head to lunch." She smiled at Noah before walking away.

"Hey thanks," Riley said as the pair walked back to the locker room.

"No problem."

For the next two weeks, Noah settled into a routine. He went to school and Riley taught him board games. He didn't see too much of Elise or Jamal except when they passed him in the halls, during gym, or at lunch. They were too busy hanging around the older kids, which he understood.

Noah was even beginning to like Miss Dawson's class. Learning from the tablet and from her personally was enjoyable. All classes should be like that. Noah didn't even draw that much during her class, and he especially didn't try to access his power.

Noah was looking at his tablet when a notification popped up.

NOAH, PLEASE HEAD TO THE OFFICE.

"Miss Dawson," he said, raising his hand. "I got this...thing on my tablet."

She checked her own tablet. "Oh yes. The school will sometimes send things like "go see the doctor" or "you have a phone call." It's far more efficient than having a runner barge in and interrupt class. Don't you agree?"

No. But Noah nodded.

"I'll see you when you come back, and we can go over the math lesson again, OK?" Miss Dawson smiled and Noah returned it.

Noah stepped outside the classroom and was startled by a familiar face.

"Hello, Noah," Mr. Cooper said. "Sorry to pull you out of class, but I wanted to see how you were doing after your first month."

"I'm doing OK."

"Nonsense. I hear you're doing great. I knew you'd fit right in."

Noah put his hands in his pockets and shrugged. "It hasn't been long."

"You don't give yourself enough credit," Mr. Cooper said. "You're way more advanced with your powers than even the older kids. And you've helped Riley, something we were not able to do. Plus I hear you're not having any trouble in school." He stopped. "To be honest, I thought you might have a little trouble academically. Your grades at your old school weren't the best. Sam will be glad to know his innovative learning techniques are working." Mr. Cooper waved his hands. "But we've had plenty of worse students. That's not why you're here, after all."

Mr. Cooper smiled. "I'm glad I was right about you, Noah. You'll make a fine student here at the school and learn more about your powers. You've not yet unlocked your full potential."

"What do you mean?"

Mr. Cooper had a sly smile on his face but didn't answer.

Noah was surprised that Mr. Cooper had led them to the front of the school. He was nervous as they walked by the sentry guarding it. It turned its gaze on him.

"I think you're going to like this," Mr. Cooper said, opening the front door.

What else is there?

Noah stopped and a huge smile crossed his face.

"Mom! Dad!" He rushed to his parents and ran into their arms.

"Ooof!" Dad said. "Careful, son. You've only been gone two weeks."

"Enough of that." Mom bent down and stroked her son's hair. "I don't care if he's been gone two weeks or an hour, I still miss my baby."

Noah normally hated it when his parents smothered him. "I'm so glad to see you," Noah said. "It's been rough at the school."

"What do you mean?" Dad asked. "Mr. Cooper said you've been doing great and thought we should surprise you. They don't normally do this."

"It's..." Noah paused, glancing back at Mr. Cooper. "It's tough living in a dorm room. I didn't realize how tough it would be. I've always had my own room. So many noises and so many people. It makes it hard to sleep."

"Oh that," Dad said.

"You'll get used to it," Mom said. "Remember your Aunt Lisa and Aunt Zee? There was a time when all three of us had to share a room together. Worst years of my life."

"That's because Zee won't ever stop talking," Dad said. "I'm sure she talks in her sleep."

Mom snorted. "That's true."

"Mr. and Mrs. Noble," Mr. Cooper said. "You haven't much time."

"Oh, we better get going," Dad said. "Thanks again."

"Any time. We're grateful to have Noah enrolled at our school. Just please don't be late."

"Where are we going?" Noah asked.

"The school said we can take you out to an early lunch. We have an hour. You'll miss gym, but it's just gym."

"I like gym," Noah said.

"You do?" Mom said.

Noah nodded. But he wasn't thinking about his fellow classmates' powers. Right now he was thinking about Riley. How would Riley handle gym without him?

"Come on, son," Dad said. "Tell me all about how you like gym now." He put his arm around Noah and whispered, "And maybe you can also tell me if you've met any girls."

"James," Mom said, rolling her eyes.

The family left the School of Expressive and Extraordinary Young People and drove to a nearby diner. Noah answered his parents' questions about the new school, but his mind was somewhere else. It was with Riley, Elise, and even Jamal.

As they had lunch, Noah thought about telling his parents everything. He didn't. With all the powers Noah had seen, he thought they might be watching him or listening. He rubbed the back of his neck where the device was. But worse still, his parents might think he was a freak if they found out what he could do. Instead, he enjoyed the moment with his parents, as a young boy should, and left out everything to do with robotic sentries, kids with powers, and a gym full of training.

When they arrived back at the school, Noah hugged his parents even more tightly.

"We should have sent you to a private school earlier," Dad said. "It would have made you miss us even more."

"Shush," Mom said. She ran her fingers through Noah's afro, trying to make it even. "Ugh. I wish they would have made you get rid of this thing."

"I like it. It's part of his heritage."

"Don't get me started on your pictures from when you were a kid." Mom smiled at Noah. "We're here if you need us. Mr. Cooper said you can call us once a week, so I expect regular phone calls. And keep up the good work in school." She pinched his cheeks. "I'm so proud of you."

"And I want you to tell me about all the pretty girls here," Dad said. "Speaking of which, I almost forgot." He pulled out a piece of paper from his back pocket. "Mika wanted me to give this to you.

Noah opened it.

Stay strong.

-M and J

"Awww, isn't that cute?" Mom asked. "Your friends are worried about you. If only they knew how well you're doing at your new school. We'll be sure to tell them."

But as Noah stared at the note, he knew the real reason behind it.

"Tell them...tell them, I'm doing OK, and that I will."

Noah kissed and hugged his parents before running back to the school.

As he went inside, the sentry stared at him. Noah gave it a wide berth, afraid of what it could do and what its orders were if Noah ran back outside. The rest of the school was busy getting their lunch and eating it in the cafeteria, on the grass, wherever it was the kids felt like congregating. Noah wasn't hungry, but he should find Riley to see how he'd done during gym.

Noah rounded the bush that needed trimming. It was a great spot when it was hot, as it provided ample shade. Unfortunately, it was always taken by the older kids. He thought most of the kids were still getting their lunch, but he saw a figure sniffling.

"Excuse me," he said. The older kid stopped. "Elise? Is that you?"

The figure turned and wiped her eyes. "Noah? I heard you were out with your parents. Back already?"

"What are you doing here? What's wrong?"

Elise stood straighter and tugged at her sleeves. She smiled, but there was no light in her eyes. "Did you have fun with your parents?"

"Yeah, but—"

"Good. Hang onto that feeling. My mom left when I was young, and I was never close to my dad." Elise bent down and hugged Noah. Whispering into his ear, she said, "Be careful, Noah. The school will treat you well as long as you obey their rules and use your powers to do what they want, but as soon as you can't, t hey..."

"What, Elise? What happens?"

She looked away, unable to meet his gaze.

The talk and laughter of a group of kids approached. Noah turned to look at them, and when he turned back, Elise was gone.

For the rest of the day, Noah couldn't stop thinking about Elise. He'd have to talk to her later. But first he wanted to see how Riley did without him there.

"Hey, Riley," Noah said in the hallway. He rushed to him before lunch was over. Any second now the bell would ring.

"Hey, Noah. Heard you got off campus. How was it?"

"It was fine. My parents took me to get a burger. How was gym? Sorry I wasn't there to practice with you."

Riley shook his head. "It went fine. I was able to...control my powers a lot better than I did before." He looked up at Noah and smiled. "Thank you."

Noah returned his smile. "Hey, I gotta go. I'll see you around."

"OK."

That was one less thing Noah had to worry about, but he still worried about Elise.

Noah didn't see Elise at school for the rest of the day or during the weekend. That was no surprise. A few of the older kids were allowed to leave school on weekends. She also could have been avoiding him. But when Monday came and Noah searched for her, he still didn't find her. There was one person who might know where she was.

Noah found Jamal surrounded by other kids, talking and laughing about subjects Noah didn't understand or care about. Noah took a deep breath. He didn't much care for groups of older kids. They were like those nature shows, always in a pack, and they always made fun of him. But Noah couldn't wait forever for Jamal to be alone. Their recess was short.

"Jamal," Noah said, creeping up to the older kids.

"What does the baby want?" another kid said.

"Can it," Jamal said. He bent down and said, "What do you want, mushroom?"

"Hey, have you seen Elise around? I haven't seen her anywhere."

"She's a little old for you, small fry," a kid said and snickered.

"Among other things."

Three of the kids laughed and Jamal cracked a smile.

"Where is she, Jamal?" Noah asked.

"Calm down." Jamal and the other three kids looked at each other before Jamal shook his head. "She's around. I wouldn't worry about her."

"Jamal, let's go," a kid said, tilting his head.

"All right. Take it easy, mushroom. See you around."

Noah sighed watching the older kids leave. "All right." No matter how well Noah may be doing in school, or how good he was with his powers, outside of gym, he was just the short new kid.

After school was over and Noah had done his homework and eaten dinner, he helped clean up the kitchen. He emptied the trash, carrying the heavy black bags as well as he could in his small arms. He wrinkled his nose, doing his best not to smell it and to keep it from spilling out. He could only carry one at a time and would have to go back for the other bags. But he wasn't making the mistake he had made before. That was a mess and a stinky one at that.

Noah quickly tossed the bags into the large bins behind the kitchens, hoping that he wouldn't see any rats. A large shadow crept across the dim lighting outside. Something brushed against his shoulder and he yelped.

"Ahhh!" Noah screamed.

A hand covered his mouth. It was Jamal.

"Quiet," he said, loosening his hand. He peered around. "You never know who's listening. For a fader, you're like the worst spy ever."

"What do you want?"

"To tell you about Elise."

"I thought you said she's OK?" Noah asked.

Jamal exhaled. "You've been here a month. It's time for you to learn the truth about SEXY school. As my dad used to say, 'There's more than meets the eye.'"

"Is that from a movie?"

Jamal nodded. "Yeah, an old one. Meet me here at midnight."

"But—"

Noah wasn't trying to get in trouble. But he remembered his friends Mika and Jeff. That was why he had come to the school in the first place. And, more importantly, he was still worried about his new friend Elise. She didn't seem right and now she was missing.

Noah nodded. "I'll come."

Jamal grinned. "Good, mushroom. See you tonight. Wear black."

"What are we going to do?"

But Jamal had already walked away. There was no turning back now. Whatever Jamal was going to show him, he was going to find out.

Noah was too nervous to sleep. Yet the seconds stretched into hours. Time wouldn't move any faster no matter how much he wished for it.

When the time finally came, Noah was already dressed. He snuck out of the dorm room, past the sleeping and snoring bodies. He nearly jumped when the door creaked as he opened it. He peered out, expecting a sentry to reach out and snatch him.

There were no cameras in the dormitory, at least none that Noah could see. Yet there were plenty of cameras outside. As Noah crept to the garbage, every noise he heard, from a cricket to an airplane flying overhead, caused him to nearly jump. He hugged himself against the walls and where he thought the blind spots would be and hid against the bushes and garbage cans when he had to.

At the pace Noah moved, it took forever for him to reach the garbage. He let out a sigh of relief when he did. Yet he didn't see Jamal anywhere.

"You're late," Jamal said from behind. "I was wondering if you'd show up."

Noah stopped himself from yelling. He didn't want to give them away.

"Here, put this on." Jamal handed him a black beanie. He winced when Noah put it on. "It'll do. That hair of yours, while I like it, it sticks out. Thank God you're small."

"Where are we going?" Noah whispered. "Where's Elise?"

"Shhh. I'm going to give you what answers I can but we gotta hurry."

"What about the sentries?"

"This time of night, there's only one," Jamal said. "And it's guarding the front entrance. The rest are put in storage. They're solar powered but they require a lot of energy to function. Especially if they have to activate their gear and defenses. Right now, it's just people watching us on the cameras. They're tired and bored and prone to mistakes and can be bribed—like all people, especially adults. Follow me, be quiet, and keep your head down."

Noah nodded.

Jamal led them through the school, hugging against the walls and crouching down low. They couldn't see the cameras through the dark globes, but Jamal paused every so often. They came to an area in the back of the courtyard that Noah had never been to. There was a small shed and grass but nothing special about it.

They crouched by some bushes and Jamal said, "That's a supply shed. But there's more to it than catsup and potatoes. Come on."

Jamal darted out and Noah followed him to the shed. There were no guards or any visible cameras, but there was a lock on the wooden door. Jamal grabbed a nearby rock and hammered it in the right spot, popping the old, rusted lock free.

Jamal didn't turn the lights on, but there was enough moonlight for Noah to see. Sacks of potatoes, canned vegetables and fruit, two large refrigerators, one large freezer, and jars of catsup and mustard were inside. *What does this have to do with Elise?*

Jamal went to where the potatoes sat on the shelf. The shelf was only two feet from the floor. He moved both the potatoes and the shelf revealing a vent.

"We found this last year," Jamal said.

"We?"

"Yeah, we were looking for a way out. Instead, we found this."

"Is it a way out?"

Jamal shrugged. "Not sure. It's a tight fit down there and the kid who last went down there couldn't squeeze through."

"Is that why you wanted me to come? Because I would fit?"

Jamal shook his head. "It's not just that. There are other younger, smaller kids, but you're different, Noah."

"In what way?"

"You have balls, kid. Big ones. You're going to need that to survive here. There are...things that happen here. We gotta find out for sure what it is. We have a right to know. You up to it?"

Noah nodded.

"Good. Now get in there. We haven't much time. The guards are making their rounds across campus."

"OK."

Jamal gave Noah a small flashlight before taking back the beanie. Noah squeezed into the vent, squirming before settling in. He turned the flashlight on, peering down the dark corridor. He saw what Jamal had been talking about. It got narrow as it went along.

Noah followed it, twisting his body like a snake as he went. He didn't mind being in small, cramped places. It was the one time when his small stature gave him an advantage. Being in the vents reminded him of crawling in the crawlspace under his house. His dad wanted him to look for rats or raccoons that one time. That was disgusting. This vent was far clearer than that one had been.

"See anything?" Jamal asked, peeking inside. His voice echoed behind him.

"No, I—"

The dark vent brightened up ahead, and Noah turned off his flashlight. He crawled to it, peeking underneath.

A dozen monitors were lit up in front of a bored guard leaning back in an office chair. The monitors showed the school exterior, the courtyard, the hallways, the cafeteria, and the gym. But what stood out were the three monitors showing a white room. Noah had never seen any of these white rooms anywhere. In all three of them were students he had seen around campus, including one whose hair he recognized very wel l.

"Elise," he whispered.

The thumping in his heart grew louder. He squirmed to get a better look at her. What were she and the other students doing in these padded cells? But Noah couldn't make out what was happening to the students or see anyone else inside the cells. It was late. Of course nothing would be going on. But what happened in the daytime? He needed to find out more.

He turned away from the guard room and ventured deeper into the vent. Noah kept the flashlight off, only using the light from the vents to guide his way. He came across a janitor's closet and storage room. He yawned. It was getting late and his slow, cautious pace in the vents was taking far too long. He decided to check one more opening, and when he did, he found one of the rooms the guard watched over.

A tall boy huddled in the corner, shivering even with a thin blanket covering him. Noah recognized the boy. He had seen him around school, but didn't remember his name.

"Psst," Noah said. "Hey." The boy didn't wake.

Noah continued crawling and the next two rooms were empty. The third wasn't, and it was there he found Elise.

Elise had her knees against her chest and was huddled in the corner. Her eyes were closed, her clothes were drenched in sweat, and she rocked herself back and forth.

Noah's heart sank. *What did they do to you?*

"Elise," Noah whispered. "Hey Elise." Noah thought about yelling, but he wasn't sure if the rooms were microphoned. Right now, he didn't care. He just didn't want Elise to think she was alone.

"Elise!" Noah said loudly, but she still didn't stir from her disturbed slumber.

Noah took the flashlight and briefly shone it on her face. He did it again and again, turning it off and on in short bursts so the guard wouldn't see. Finally, she moaned and moved, slowly blinking her eyes.

"Noah?" she asked, her voice raw as she looked at him.

Noah smiled and put a finger to his lips. He was about to say something when a loud noise reverberated through the vent. Noah ached to talk to Elise more, but his fear drove him to crawl back the way he came.

"Sorry, I gotta go," he said. "I'll try to come back if I can."

The further he got, the more the tapping noise increased, beating steadily. Noah slowed down when he saw the familiar hand through the vent.

A sour face greeted Noah when he came to the vent's entrance.

"What took you so long?" Jamal asked. "I didn't mean for you to go crawling through the school's entire vent system."

Noah couldn't help but smile. "I found her! I found Elise. And there are others."

Jamal helped him from the vent. "Good. Tell me all about it while we get outta here."

While Noah told Jamal all he had seen and done, Jamal didn't seem concerned for Elise and the others trapped in there. Noah wanted to know if there was something they could do. If they could somehow rescue Elise. Jamal didn't give him a straight answer.

Even though Noah was extremely tired the next day, his mind kept going back to Elise. Maybe he didn't need Jamal to rescue her. It's not like he could fit in the vents anyway. There might be a way. Something he could find. He could do it on his own. *I wish Jeff and Mika were here.*

Noah was eating lunch with Riley in the cafeteria, trying to pay attention to Riley's words. But after last night, Noah just wasn't interested, and his weariness started to set in.

He perked up seeing that familiar strand of purple hair weaved in with the black.

"Elise?"

Noah left in the middle of Riley's sentence and bolted over to Elise, all the way on the other side of the cafeteria. She barely had time to lift her tray before he crashed into her, squeezing her legs.

"Oof!" she said, tightening up.

He looked up at her. The purple in her hair had faded and the bags were heavy under her eyes. "I'm sorry. I shouldn't have."

"It's all right." Elise held her tray and squeezed him into a hug. She bent down and kissed him on the forehead. "Let's talk later, OK?"

Noah nodded his head so hard, he looked like a bobblehead.

"Good. I'll see you later."

The school day couldn't end soon enough for Noah. He was desperate to talk to Elise. He also really wanted to crawl into bed. But first he had to do both his homework and his chores.

Noah and the other kids his age were too small to help with things like sweeping, ironing, mopping, and washing the dishes. They were assigned to carry the larger pots and pans from the sink back to the storage unit where they belonged. He struggled with a heavy pot even though it was empty.

"Need some help?" a familiar voice said from behind.

He turned around and grinned. "Elise!" He ached to hug her but couldn't with the pot in his arms.

"Let me take that for you." She lifted the pot with ease.

The pair slowly walked to the cabinets.

"Elise, what—"

"Not here, not now."

Elise put the pot down before dragging Noah by the arm. She led him behind the kitchen and in between two large bushes. A couple of teenagers were there kissing and fondling each other.

"Out," Elise said, her tone flat. One of them opened their mouth. "Now!"

The teenagers left, giving Elise an evil glare.

Once they were gone, Elise exhaled and clenched her teeth together. "Noah, you need to be more careful at this school. How did you find me?"

Noah told her about Jamal and his plan and what Noah had found when he crawled through the vents.

"Jamal," she said, rolling her eyes. Her eyes focused on Noah again. "I wish he didn't drag you into whatever scheme he has. There's more going on at this school than you know. I was there for a...reason."

"Why? What did they do to you? It didn't look like any good reason to me."

Elise didn't look at him as she answered. "You're special, Noah. I suppose we all are. But you're far more advanced than most of us. You can use your ability in a way that took a few of us years, and most of us can't even go that far. And you even helped Riley when some of us thought he was beyond help."

"I don't get it. What does that have to do with what they did to you?"

Elise bent down and gently set her hand on his shoulder. "Whatever you think this school is, forget it. They only care about one thing—our abilities and how it will serve them. They've treated you well, not because you're young and new but because of what you can do." Elise paused, biting her lip and tugging on her long sleeve. She looked at her feet, and in a quiet voice, said, "And some of us can only go so far, no matter how long we've been here and how hard we've tried. That's not good enough for them."

"Elise, I—" Noah reached up to her face to wipe away a tear, and she spun around and stormed off.

Noah had no idea where she was going but he chased after her. He wanted to make sure she was all right. There had to be something else he could do to help.

She brought them to the gym. Jamal wiped down the mats, and Elise stormed straight toward him.

Jamal looked up and grinned. "Come to help?"

Elise balled up her fist and struck Jamal. He crumpled to the ground, blood leaking from his nose. Elise readied to strike him again when Noah jumped in the way.

"You bitch!" Jamal yelled, pinching his nose. "What the hell did you do that for?"

Noah struggled to push the two taller teenagers away from each other as best as he could.

Elise pointed her finger at Jamal. "Don't use Noah like that again! You knew what could happen if he got caught!"

"Bah. You underestimate the little mushroom. Besides, he was worried about what was happening to you, unlike most of us here."

Elise narrowed her eyes at Jamal. "Why don't you tell him the *real* reason you wanted him to go down there."

Noah looked up at Jamal. *What does she mean?*

Jamal glanced away and scratched the back of his head. He shrugged. "If you think he's old enough to handle it. Fine." He turned to Noah, rubbing his nose. "Years ago, before the sentries arrived and the devices were implanted in us, there were stories of kids escaping. But since the school built those machines and stuck us with these—things—no kids have escaped. No kids except for one.

"About two summers ago, there was a fader. Quiet kid like yourself. I don't know, maybe it runs in you guys. Anyway, he mostly kept to himself. Didn't make waves or get into trouble. Didn't make any friends either." Jamal shrugged. "I didn't pay too much attention to him. Why would I?"

"Get to the point, Jamal," Elise said.

"All right, all right," he said, rolling his eyes. "Anyway, as the story goes, we were in the gym practicing our powers when the kid faded. No one even knew he was gone. Back then they didn't do a count after class like they do now."

"But they had devices that track us and control our powers?" Noah asked, rubbing the back of his neck.

Jamal nodded. "Oh yeah. But the sentries were still new. There were only two and they weren't in the gym with us. The kid just vanished. They locked down the school, but no one's ever seen him again. After that, things became stricter with the increased security measures."

"But how did he do it?" Noah asked. "How did he get past the devices in our necks?"

"Don't know. That's up to you to find out."

"Me?"

Elise stepped between the two. "OK, story time is over. Tell him."

"I think you can help us escape," Jamal said. "You're brave, smart, and your powers are the key."

"But I don't know how to do what he did."

"Maybe not," Jamal said. "But you're smart enough to find a way."

Noah opened his mouth but Jamal stopped him.

"Look, we don't all want to be here," Jamal said, gripping the mop's handle. "Some of us have family and friends we'd like to see, even if they're two states over. You're lucky. Your family's here. They even allow you to see them because you're doing so well. But let me tell you something. When you don't do well, they give you the stick like they did to Elise."

Elise tugged on her sleeves and looked away.

"If you hadn't helped Riley," Jamal said, "who knows how they would have reacted? You already have talent and skill in using your power, but they're going to push you. Give it time. They're gonna want to see how far you can take your powers."

Noah stared at Elise and Jamal. The older kids didn't say a word. Noah didn't want to try to escape. That wasn't the plan. The plan was to collect information and find out more about the school and his powers. But Noah thought about how Riley had suffered during gym when he first met him and about how Elise's eyes were full of sadness. While he liked the idea of a school existing to help kids learn their powers, people shouldn't be forced to attend or be tortured if they couldn't do it. He remembered Mr. Cooper's words about there being more to his abilities. *Would they force me to reach that level? And what happens if I can't?*

But this wasn't about him and his abilities. This was about his new friends and the other kids in the school.

"I'll do it," Noah said, looking directly at Elise. "I make no promises, but I'll help you escape if I can."

"Yes!" Jamal said. "I knew it!" He clapped Noah on the back.

"I'll help you, but don't ever disrespect Elise again." Noah turned and walked away from them.

CHAPTER 17

NOAH HAD SAID he'd help them, and he would, but he wasn't sure how. It had been over two weeks, and he still wasn't any closer to helping them escape. In all their time together, though Jamal had said the previous fader's power was the key, he hadn't said how or why. The pair had provided him with a layout of the school, which Noah had expertly drawn on paper. But getting past the device in his neck was entirely up to Noah.

He squeezed the pencil in his hand. *If only I could practice my power outside of gym.*

"You've been distracted lately," Riley said, sitting down next to him on the grassy hill.

"I have?"

"You do realize I can feel your emotions in gym class?"

"Yeah, sorry. I've just had a lot on my mind."

"I can tell," Riley said. "And it has to do with those two."

Noah followed Riley's gaze toward Elise and Jamal.

"You've been spending a lot of time with them lately," he said.

"They're my friends," Noah said. "I'm just glad Elise is back. I was worried about her. Do you know what they do to the kids here?"

Riley sighed. "I know."

"You know?"

He nodded. "Yes. Things aren't as bad as Jamal and Elise and the older kids make it out to be."

"But Elise—"

"She wasn't the only one who had to go to that part of the school we call The Dungeon. But they do it for our own good." Riley looked away and his voice grew quieter. "Before you met me, things were far worse. I'd scream and yell. I was a five-year-old throwing a tantrum. They helped me, Noah, and they can help

Elise too if she'd just give them a chance. The school can be tough, but they do it for our own good. They can help us and you'll know that as soon as you accept that you belong here and become a part of the school."

Riley rose and dusted off the grass that clung to his pant legs. "Now come on. We don't wanna be late for class."

Noah put away his notebook and drawing, watching Riley run off.

Troi leaned on the doorway, smacking the gum in her mouth until she blew a large bubble.

"You ready?" she asked.

"Uh-huh." Noah nodded.

Troi was one of the older kids that Jamal had put him in contact with. She worked in the kitchens just like Noah did. Jamal thought she might help Noah with a plan he came up with. He wanted to sneak into the nurse's office and turn off the devices, or at least sabotage the one in his neck, so he could practice using his powers outside of gym. And Troi had proved a willing ally. Not everyone agreed or even liked Noah's plan. But with the help of Jamal and Elise, they had been able to convince a few to help him.

Noah struggled to match Troi's long strides. She stopped to look at him. "Try to keep up. We haven't much time."

He pushed his legs to catch up with her but always trailed. "I know. I know."

They reached the hallways and paused. "Come on, let's—"

She pushed him against the wall. "Wait!" Footsteps vibrated through the hallway. Noah's heart pounded. It slowed down when the steps receded.

Troi smacked her gum again. "I hope this is worth it."

The pair crept to the nurse's door, peering around on the lookout for anyone. Noah gasped, staring at the black strip. The only way to open it was to have a key card, and he wasn't sure that either Troi or Jamal had access to one.

"Are you sure you can get us in?" Noah asked.

Troi cocked her head. "Are you sure your plan will work?"

No. But he didn't say so out loud. If only he could use his powers like the previous kid.

"How can you get us in without your powers?" Noah asked.

Troi pulled out a small tool kit and started working on the lock. "I love puzzles. My dad and I used to work on them all the time. He said I would make a great engineer one day." Troi softly smiled. She stopped smiling and a hard gaze fell upon Noah.

"They might study us, cage us, and dissect us, but they'll never understand us," she said. "Jamal convinced me to do this because I have an ability to break into any lock. I can see how they work and solve it. They might be able to turn off our powers, but they'll always be a part of us no matter what they do. Just because I can't access my powers doesn't mean they're not a part of me."

Noah thought about her words and stared at his hands. *She might be right.* There was so much about his powers Noah didn't understand.

A rumbling noise vibrated under Noah's feet. He grabbed Troi's arm, getting ready to run.

"Wait," she said.

A couple of teenagers ran past them, excited looks on their faces.

"It's about time," Troi said. "Jamal sure took his sweet time. Come on."

Troi finished breaking the lock to the nurse's office. The black key reader hung dangling off the door.

"Without my powers," she said, "it's not as smooth as it'd normally be. They're going to know we were here. Let's hurry."

The pair went into the office. Noah wrapped his arms around himself and shivered, staring at the chair where he'd sat on his first day. If only he had known what they were going to do to him. He shrugged. He probably couldn't have stopped them even if he had known.

Noah and Troi rummaged through the office, going through the drawers, cabinets, and computers. They looked for the needles that had been stuck into them on the first day of school. They looked for the little chips that were now in their bodies. But they didn't find anything.

"Noah, did you see anything when you were first here? Someplace where Nurse Ratchet would have put it?"

Noah cupped his chin under his finger, thinking about it. No, he hadn't. She'd snuck up behind him and stuck him with it.

Troi snorted. "I told Jamal this was a waste of time. We—" Troi fell silent and perked her head up. "Did you hear that?"

"What?"

"Shhh! There it is again."

Noah focused and heard a rhythmic thumping. The steady sound grew louder and closer.

"Shit!" Troi said. "Thought Jamal would have given us a better diversion and we'd have a little more time."

"What is it?" Noah asked, looking at the doorway.

"It's the sentries. They can't mimic humans that well. They walk like horror movie villains. Hide!"

Noah ducked under the table and squeezed himself into a ball as best he could. The thumping stopped, and he glimpsed the sentries' long legs from underneath the table.

"Designation Troi Diego," the sentry said. "You do not belong here."

"That's me!" she said with perk in her voice.

"You do not belong here. Come with me."

"And if I don't?"

The sentry's long legs stiffened and took a step forward. Noah held his breath. *What can they do?*

"OK, OK, I'll come," she said. "Jeez, I was just looking for something for my headache."

Noah waited until they were gone, slowly peeking out of the room. Once it was clear, he ran out of the room searching for either Elise or Jamal.

Noah found Elise behind the storage shed outside of the cafeteria.

"There you are!" she said. "I was worried about you. I saw the sentry take Troi, and thought it had you too."

Noah shook his head then told her all about it. "What happened with Jamal and the distraction? We thought—"

"It wasn't nearly distracting enough," Jamal said, walking to join them. He rubbed his face. A dark bruise was there. "Did your plan work? Did you find a way to disable the devices in our necks?"

Noah sighed. "Sorry, we couldn't find anything and we didn't have enough time."

Jamal glowered at him. "You mean I got this bruise for nothing?"

Elise snorted a laugh. "Not for nothing."

Jamal looked at her sideways. "I told you guys this was a waste of time. Mushroom. Noah, it's up to you. Devices or not, you're the one with the power to get rid of them during gym."

"But what if I find a way to escape first and then—"

"We've been over this!" Jamal said. "If I had hair like yours, I'd be pulling it out right now." Jamal stormed off in frustration, muttering to himself.

Noah watched him. His shoulders dropped as if he had the weight of the world on his shoulders. Maybe the other fader had been smarter and more powerful than he was. He couldn't do anything right.

Elise bent down and grabbed Noah by the shoulders. "Noah," she said in a soft voice. "Don't listen to Jamal. He's an ass almost all the time. This isn't about him. This isn't about me or any of the others. This is about you. If the other kid could do it, you can. You're one of the most skilled freaks here."

She gave him a warm smile and Noah tried to return it. But then her sleeves slid back, and Noah stared at the marks on her arms. Elise caught his gaze and pulled her arms back, turning away.

"Don't worry, Noah. We'll think of something." She ran off in the opposite direction from Jamal.

As Noah watched her go, he remembered her arms and the hope that had been in her and Jamal's eyes.

She's wrong. It was not about him. It was about the other kids here. Noah needed to help them.

CHAPTER 18

A FEW DAYS later, Noah was in the gym again. He hadn't thought of any more plans, and neither had Jamal or Elise. But maybe the older kids were right—maybe it had been inside him all along. He just had to figure out how to access it.

As Noah sat cross-legged on the mat, he thought about how his powers worked. He thought about what Elise had said, what Troi had said, and even what Jamal had said. He was missing something.

When Noah used his powers, it was more than people forgetting about him. Even cameras didn't register his presence. *That means I do more than disappear.*

When Noah faded, he didn't feel a part of this world. And maybe that was it. The device they had implanted in him wasn't a part of Noah either.

Noah closed his eyes and accessed his power. But he didn't use it. Instead, he held onto it as long as he could, feeling like he held the link between worlds. Instead of letting his entire body access it, he focused on the device in his neck. On how he had felt the first time it was injected. How sometimes it itched and it never felt quite right.

This is it.

Noah focused all the power within him like a laser, smashing it into the back of his neck where the device was. The device was pushed out of his neck. No, Noah faded from it.

The sentry's eyes lit up and focused its attention on Noah. *Now's my chance.* Noah let his body fade from the world around him.

"Designation: Noah Nobles," the sentry said in a robotic and flat voice. Yet its words were no less threatening. "You are to cease activity and report to the nearest teacher immediately."

The students around Noah stopped their training and he ducked between them, using them as shields, to no advantage. The sentry stalked him, pushing through kids. If the sentry reached Noah, it would be too late.

A ball of blur smashed into the sentry, knocking it off balance. A kid with wild hair smiled and winked. "Sorry."

The sentry looked at the student before turning its gaze back to Noah. Its long footsteps continued striding toward him.

A small girl stomped her foot on the mats. The mats erupted, rolling like tidal waves and smashing into the sentry.

"Noah, now!" Jamal yelled. "Get outta here!"

Noah ran through the throng of students as most of them converged on the sentry. The plan among the three was that Jamal and Elise would get as many students as they could to attack and distract the sentry while Noah made his escape.

Far more students than Noah had expected attacked the sentry—about a third of the students in the school. One turned into a thick green goo, smothering the sentry. The sentry heated up. Fumes of steam rose from it and the goo melted away. An older teenager blew into his thumb and it ballooned into a massive fist. He smacked it into the sentry, sending it crashing into the wall.

Noah's and Jamal's eyes met. "What did I say? Go!"

Noah sprinted out of the gym, not daring to look back at his fellow classmates even though their cries rang in his ears. Noah rushed outside, sprinting to the storage room. Noah rubbed the back of his neck where his implant would be, scratching an invisible sensation. It was only a matter of time before they activated the devices in the student's necks.

The school bell chimed. "All students are to remain where they are."

It wouldn't be long before the sentries closed in on him.

A long leg stepped out into the courtyard. Noah quickly ducked behind a bush and quietly waited. He only breathed when the sentry veered off in the direction of the gym.

Noah reached the storage room, slipped inside, and leaned against the doorway. His heart thumped in his chest, but he had to remember why he was doing this. He exhaled at the grate on the floor.

The grate was far larger and heavier to move without Jamal. It seemed to take Noah forever to lift it and get inside, and even longer to put it back. But this was the plan. The vents were the only place that wasn't monitored and were too small for the sentries to fit inside.

As soon as he scraped the grate back into place, the door to the storage shed slammed open. Noah froze not far from the opening. He held his breath, thankful that he had spent the extra time closing the vent. Heavy footsteps approached him, and a large shadow hovered over the vent's opening.

Please don't see me. Please don't see me. Please don't see me.

Noah squeezed his eyes shut tightly and didn't move. He had no idea what the sentries could do. They could see him even when he used his powers. Could they also track him? Could they see his footprints as he fled the gym?

The robot's heavy steps receded and Noah allowed himself to open his eyes and breathe again. He peered into the vent, wishing he had a flashlight. He took a deep breath. There was no turning back now. He crawled deeper into the vents.

He went by the security guard. This time he was wide awake, talking on a radio, scanning the monitors as they looked for Noah. If it hadn't been so serious, he might have found it funny. He knew that one direction led to the cells, so he shimmied down in another direction, hoping it led to a way out.

Noah continued crawling. He inched his way down but shook his head in resignation when it led to a dead end. He shimmed around and crawled, picking an offshoot vent he had passed.

He paused and blew into his sweat-filled hands. It was so cold in there, and his hands felt as if he'd be crawling around for hours.

"Finally," he said, seeing light at the end of one vent. He crawled to it and peeked out, greeted by the bright tiles on the floor and familiar toilet below him.

He turned around, away from the bathroom. He was trying to get out of school, not back into it.

The dust began creeping into Noah's nose. He raised his head and slammed it into the bathroom ceiling as he sneezed. He rubbed his head, feeling a growing bump. He just wanted out of this stupid school already. But Jamal and Elise were wrong. There didn't seem to be a way out through these vents.

No. He couldn't think that way. He had to at least find a way out, no matter how long it took.

Hope rose in Noah as he spotted sunlight. Since his eyes had gotten used to the dim lighting of the fluorescent lights, the bright sunlight nearly blinded him when he reached it. He found himself behind the school, in the loading docks where the school received shipments. A few trucks were there right now. If only he could break free, he could get out of here.

Noah pushed against the grate but it didn't budge. He grabbed it and pushed but it still didn't move. He slammed his fist against it. He glanced down the way he had come. There were other ways that might lead him out, but they might also take him deeper into the school. There was no way of knowing, and he couldn't stay here forever.

Aaaaah!

The delivery trucks were starting their engines and driving away. The driver closest to Noah was about to get into his truck when an idea came to him. He took a deep breath and calmed himself.

"Help!" Noah said. The man paused and looked around. "Help!" Noah prayed this worked; otherwise, he would alert the school to his position.

The man cautiously turned around and slowly approached Noah. Noah stuck out his lip, trying his best to look as sad as he could. He wiped his face with the dirt lying in the vent and closed his eyes hard, willing tears to come out of them.

The man crouched down. "What are you doing in there?" He grabbed the vent, but it didn't move. "Let me get you some help."

"No!" Noah shouted. "Please. They put me in here in the first place." Noah grabbed the vent tighter, praying that his desperate look would convince this stranger to help him.

The man furrowed his brow. He glanced at the side of the grate and said, "I'll be back."

Noah stiffened, worried that the man would change his mind and notify someone in the school. Instead, he came back with tools and proceeded to unscrew the vent. Noah crawled out and allowed himself a moment of relief as he breathed in the fresh air and the sunshine crawled on his skin. "Thank you."

Noah walked away when the man grabbed him by the arm.

"Now wait a minute," he said. "I need to take you to someone to get some help. See what's going on. There's some kind of commotion and we've been ordered to leave. I haven't even finished my delivery, and my boss isn't going to be happy."

Noah thought about telling him about the school and what they did. How he might be in danger just for helping Noah or asking questions. Instead, when the man bent down to pick up his tools, Noah faded.

"Where'd he go?" the man said, his eyes, scanning the area. He sighed. "Stupid kid. Probably got into some kind of trouble he shouldn't of."

The delivery driver loaded his tools and got back in his truck. As he drove away, he didn't know that he carried with him an extra load.

CHAPTER 19

NOAH RUBBED his shoulders and blew into his hands. Winter hadn't come but, judging from the chill, it crept closer. He was freezing because he had run away from the school in his gym clothes. He could have easily stolen a jacket, but he wasn't going to do that.

It took Noah far too long to leave the city and go back to his town. He took trains and hid on buses, all while using his powers.

He was exhausted now. He had used up a lot of his power making the trip. He had never used his power for so long. The exercises during school had helped him, and he didn't dare reappear. With all the people in the city, he was always so scared that one of the agents or sentries would see him.

He used his power now, waiting against the brush. He had almost waited near the door, but he had decided against it. Noah just hoped the path he had chosen would be the one she took. After all, he had only been to her apartment once.

A tall, slim figure skipped on the sidewalk. Noah thought he'd be able to whisper to her, but with her earbuds in, that wasn't going to happen. He yanked her arm, reeling her in. She screamed and he defaded his head.

"Shhh! Mika, it's me!"

"Noah!" she said, pulling out her earbuds. She slowly reached out to his face. "You can make certain body parts disappear now?"

"Oh," he said, looking down. "I guess I can. My abilities have grown. I learned it in school. We need to talk. Can you and Jeff meet me at our spot as soon as possible? I've got a bunch of stuff to tell you guys. And can you have Jeff bring me a change of clothes and some food? I'm starving and cold."

Noah glanced around, afraid that by revealing himself, he'd allow the agents from the school to see him.

He faded before he received an answer, hoping his friend would come through.

Noah crouched in the tall grass, still using his powers and being as still as possible. Would his friends come and, more importantly, would they come alone?

Noah tried to still his ragged breathing. Ever since his escape from school, he had used his powers non-stop. He couldn't hold it much longer. Sweat covered his body but he didn't move.

Just a little longer. He sighed. *Finally.*

He spotted Mika and Jeff running to the tent with bags in tow. As much as he wanted to release his power, Noah didn't greet them. Not yet. He stayed still, keeping an eye out to see if they were being followed. His body cried out to release his power.

The two went into the tent, calling his name. It wasn't until they came back out that Noah made a decision.

Noah dragged his feet to them, releasing his power. "Hi." He tried to smile, collapsing to the ground.

"Hey," Jeff said, "I've got you." His friend caught him and he was grateful.

"Thanks."

"What's wrong?"

"Tired," Noah said. "Water." He smacked his mouth and saliva clung to his lips.

"Here," Mika said, getting him a bottle of water.

"Thanks."

Mika and Jeff had worried looks in their eyes. They didn't say anything; they just continued to pass glances between them.

"It's OK," Noah said once he had drunk the entire bottle of water. "I'm all right."

Jeff grinned. "That's good, little buddy." He hugged him. "I've missed you."

"*We've* missed you," Mika said, also hugging him.

"Thanks guys." As Noah allowed himself to be in their embraces, he realized how much he had missed them. It had only been almost two months, but he not only had to deal with kids older than he was, he had to wear a uniform. The kids at the School of Expressive and Extraordinary Young People had powers. Jeff and Mika didn't, and they liked him for who he was. Big hair and all.

The trio broke apart and Jeff said, "Now that we got that out of the way, can you *please* tell us what's going on? I'm dying over here."

"Yeah, we know it's big," Mika said. "And Jeff wouldn't stop bugging me with questions. And it drove me crazy that I couldn't tell him anything."

"Not as crazy as it drove me."

Noah nodded. It was time, and the reason he'd come to his friends, after all. He needed their help. There was no one he trusted more, although part of him worried that the more they knew, the more they would be in trouble with the school.

They huddled inside the tent. Noah snacked on chips and crackers as he spent the rest of the day telling his friends what he had been up to at the school and all that he had seen. He told them about the friends he'd made at school, the teachers, the sentries, and, more importantly, what he'd had seen the night he'd tried to rescue Elise.

When Noah finished, his friends were quiet for several long moments. Finally, Jeff reached into the bag and pulled out a store-bought cookie. "Wow," Jeff said. "That...that was quite a story." He ran his fingers through his hair before taking a bite of his cookie.

"When we said get intel," Mika said, "we didn't mean for you to find a secret dungeon." She laid a hand on Noah's shoulder and smiled. "But I'm glad you're OK."

Noah placed his hand on hers. The heat in his face rose as he stared into her light green eyes, amplified by her large glasses. He quickly snatched his hand back and looked away.

"What do we do now?" Jeff asked. "You know they're coming for you."

"I promised my friends at the school I'd find a way to help them.

"You're going to do this whether we help you or not," Mika said.

"Yeah."

Mika rolled her eyes. "You make it sound so easy. We're going to need a plan."

"So...you're in?" Noah asked.

"Of course we're in," Mika said. "But let's not rush it." She picked up her backpack. "I'll think of some things, but let's meet back tomorrow and work on a plan."

"Yeah!" Jeff said.

Mika frowned. "Don't sound too excited. This isn't like the movies."

"Yeah?" Jeff said in a quiet voice, shrugging. Noah couldn't help but grin.

They were about to do the impossible, but with his friends by his side, Noah didn't think it would be anything but a success.

"Glad to have you back, little buddy," Jeff said.

"Yeah, me too."

"We'll see you tomorrow. Same time," Mika said. She went to the exit and paused. "It's really good to have you back."

Noah smiled at her as she left. She was smarter than either he or Jeff was. He knew she could come up with some kind of plan to rescue the others.

Noah dressed in the clothes Jeff had brought. It was nice to wear shorts and a shirt again, even if they were a little baggy. Jeff had even brought him a sweater, although Noah had to roll up the sleeves. He settled in for the night, feeling more relaxed than he had in the entire time at the school. There were still his parents to worry about. He would have to see if his friends could check on them and maybe leave them a note. He wasn't sure what the school would do to them.

There was one other person he thought he could trust with his secret. Noah dug into his pocket, taking out the wrinkled paper he had saved from his teacher, Ms. Vera. He read her address and number. She didn't live too far from here. Maybe he should see her? He crushed the paper back into his pocket. He'd ask his friends what they thought first.

Noah fidgeted as he waited in the tent the next day. School was over. So it should only take them half an hour to get back. Yet they were already fifteen minutes late. Maybe they were carrying supplies for Noah or tools for the plan. Noah had a few ideas himself. He couldn't sit still yet he didn't feel like drawing. Too much was at stake. He left the tent and went outside to look for his friends and get some fresh air.

Noah peered out into the grass. He remembered to breathe, knowing that his friends wouldn't let him down and that they would come. *But what if something happened to them?*

"There they are," Noah said, peering out into the distance. But as the figure came into view, the person was far too tall to be any one of his friends. She wore a black suit and dark sunglasses to match, with long blond hair draped across her shoulders.

"Ms. Luna."

"Noah," she said, raising her voice. "Quite a little hideout you have here." She stopped about twenty feet away and looked over him and at the tent and surrounding area. "Impressive, really. My brother made a pillow fort once. We never had a backyard, not with our small apartment. I've always been a city girl. Camped once. Hated it."

Noah bit the inside of his cheek but said nothing.

Ms. Luna softened her voice and bent down to his height. *I hate it when they do that.* "Why don't you come with me back to the school and this will all be over."

He took a step back.

"Nothing will happen to you except detention. I promise."

"I've seen what they do to those who don't work out, like Elise."

Ms. Luna sighed and tied her hair back. "Look, they've told me that nothing like that will happen to you. I've been down there when I was younger. What you don't understand is that they put kids down there who can't control their abilities. You clearly can. And you're smart enough to have escaped from school. I couldn't control my powers as well as you at your age." She shrugged. "Who knows? Maybe one day you'll do what I do. The school's trying to help people. You haven't been there long enough to see how the school can help people."

Is that what they're trying to do, or are Elise and Jamal right? He needed more time to think. He needed someone he could trust. He needed his family or friends.

She bent down and in a soft voice said, "Why don't you just stop fading and we can go back to the school. I'll even get you some ice cream somewhere."

Fading. Noah hadn't realized he was still doing it. *Why doesn't she just use her timestop and force me to go with her?* Noah's eyes widened. That's because she can't. It might have been the distance, or it might have been the fact that Noah was still fading. She might be able to see him, but her powers couldn't affect him while he was fading.

Noah had made a promise to both of his groups of friends. He wasn't going to break that promise.

He turned and ran.

"Damn it, Noah!" she screamed. "Come back here!"

He took off through the small forest. He heard Ms. Luna run after him, her long legs gaining ground on him. Loud snaps of branches breaking ran through his ears. Noah didn't dare look back. If he did, she would catch him. The grass rustled closer to him as he went. A fallen log was about six feet from him. He slid under it instead of climbing over it as that would take far longer. The bog clung to his clothes, dirtying him, but he didn't mind. All that mattered was getting away. But Noah had been away so long that he had forgotten how the mud clutched you, sucking you into its grasp.

By the time Noah emerged from the mud, Ms. Luna had grabbed the back of his hoodie. He grunted as she pulled it.

"Let me go!" Noah yelled, pulling with all his might.

He slipped from her grasp and continued to run. Ms. Luna yelped as she got caught in the muck. Noah was almost out of the forest. Just past the bushes was the other side of the block. But he still had to get somewhere safe until he could find Mika and Jeff. Maybe he could make it to his teacher. She lived close to here.

Noah cleared the bushes, popping out on the other side and onto the sidewalk. He glanced right and left. *Which way to go?* He didn't want to lead her back to his parents' or friends' houses, but he needed a place to hide. Noah chose left and sprinted down the sidewalk, running as fast as his short legs could carry him.

His breathing became ragged and he knew he was slowing down. He veered off into the street, a car honking its horn as it passed. Noah glanced back, seeing that blond hair not far off.

"Ooof!

Fear struck him as he glanced up seeing an eyeful of blond hair. Had she somehow gotten past him?

"You all right?" She pulled out her earbuds and said, "Noah?"

He blinked and smiled. He had found her. It was Ms. Vera.

"What are you doing here?"

Noah gulped down air. "Please, Ms. Vera, you gotta help me. There's someone chasing me and—"

"Finally," Ms. Luna said. She bent down, leaning over. "I hate running, especially in this suit. Thank you for stopping."

"What's going on here?" Ms. Vera said, stepping between Noah and the agent.

"Be careful! She's dangerous!"

Ms. Luna grinned. "Kids." She stood up and dusted off her jacket. "You're a teacher from his school, right?

Noah here has run away from the school. He's actual-ly one of our best students, but he must be homesick, which is understandable. No matter how much he's excelling, he's still young. We want to have him back. We've been looking all over."

Ms. Vera looked at him. "Noah, is this true? Did you run away from school?"

"Yeah, but, you don't get it. It's not a normal school."

"He's right," Ms. Luna said. "We're a little more experimental. We don't teach the same way you public schools or even the private schools do."

"No!" Noah said, shaking his head. He hid behind his old teacher, peeking out from one side to anoth-er. "You don't understand. The school's not normal. It's..." Noah paused and looked at his teacher.

What should I tell her? She turned around. As he stared into her soft, kind eyes, which he had gotten to know over the years, he couldn't help but wonder how his beloved teacher would react to finding out that there was a world where kids have powers like in the movies.

If he couldn't trust Ms. Vera, who he had known most of his life, then who could he trust?

Noah took a deep breath and said, "There's a school where they all have powers, including me, and they train us to use our powers. But if we step out of line, they torture us."

Ms. Vera glanced down at Noah with a questioning look before turning her attention to Ms. Luna. "Is what Noah says true?"

Ms. Luna barked out laughter. "You don't actually believe this. He's a kid and an artist with a wild imagination."

Ms. Vera smiled and Noah's heart sank. "You're right, of course. It is ridiculous."

"You see, I—"

"No," Ms. Vera said, her smile disappearing. "I find it ridiculous how you use a school of children to do your bidding...*agent.*"

Noah grabbed at Ms. Vera's leg, urging her to run before Ms. Luna used her timestop ability.

Ms. Vera didn't budge and the next thing Noah saw was Ms. Luna collapsing on the sidewalk. Ms. Vera stared at Ms. Luna for several seconds with a stern look on her face. He had never seen that look before, not even when Monty acted up in class.

"Come on, Noah. Let's go back to my place."

She didn't wait for Noah to follow her, jogging back the way she had come.

Noah glanced in the other direction, where his friends lived. He had made a plan to meet up with them. What if something happened to them? What if Ms. Luna or Mr. Cooper captured them and forced them to talk?

Ms. Vera paused and looked back at Noah from twenty feet away. She didn't say a word. Just waited for him to make a decision, just like she had in class when there was a difficult math problem or a science experiment he couldn't quite understand.

He jogged to Ms. Vera. He had come to her for help. *There's no turning back now.*

CHAPTER 20

MS. VERA RENTED the bottom house in a neighborhood two blocks away. She gave Noah a glass of water as he collapsed on the sofa. It was hard to keep pace with her, but she hadn't slowed down once. He knew why. They didn't have the time. Noah had never been to her place before, but he found it odd. Unlike Mika's place, things were cleaned and well situated. But there were no pictures of her with family or friends, no movie posters or paintings, no wooden figures, not even a goldfish. It seemed sterile.

"Stay here," she said. "I need to take a quick shower and then we need to go. In my bedroom, underneath my bed, there are two large duffle bags. Can you get them for me?"

"Umm...OK."

Noah found the first bag, and while large and heavy, he managed to bring it out into the room. The second bag was the same size but heavier. He didn't want to drag it across the floor, but the weight of it caused him to drop the bag. Out of it spilled a large wad of money.

"Whoa," Noah said, gawking at the money.

The bag was full of it. He glanced back at the bathroom door, making sure Ms. Vera was still in there before hurrying and stuffing the money back inside the bag. Noah paused and opened the bag wider. Inside it was a photo. He took it out and it showed Ms. Vera, a man, and a young girl. They were all smiling and Noah had never seen Ms. Vera so happy before.

"That was my family," Ms. Vera said from behind with a damp towel in her hand. She was fully dressed but her hair was still wet.

"I'm sorry. I didn't mean to." Noah held out the photo.

"I escaped them once, and I was content to live a good life with my family before the agency took them away from me." Ms. Vera snatched the photo from Noah, stuffing it back into the bag. She sat down next to him. "You've had quite an adventure. Tell me everything you know, and leave nothing out."

While Noah wanted to know more about her, he knew that look. She meant what she said, and he would do as she asked. Maybe later he would get to ask the questions. As Noah told his story of how he got his powers, and what had happened to him since, it felt good to tell an adult the things he had seen and could do. Yet she didn't seem surprised at all by what he had said.

Ms. Vera gave him a small smile. "I knew you were special, Noah. But I thought that was in regards to drawing. I always thought your artistry would take you places. I never imagined it would be any place like this."

Her smile disappeared and her voice became somber. "You've met some very dangerous people. People I've dealt with a time or two before I came to the school. The agents want to control us or use us for their own games. When you don't fall in line, they take what you love."

Ms. Vera was quiet, staring at her hands.

"I used my powers once to help people. I...made some mistakes, but I did the best I could. The agents didn't like my methods. They believed I should work under their rules. They don't know what it's like to be one of us. Our powers are a part of us in ways that not even we fully understand."

Noah nodded and placed a gentle hand on his teacher's. "What can you do?"

Ms. Vera looked at Noah and blinked. She smiled and patted his hand. "You know, you remind me of my daughter. She would have been about your age. I can ghost. I have the ability to go into people and take over their bodies if I choose. There is a drawback. If I stay there too long, like I did with this body." Ms. Vera glanced down at her hands. "Then I become them. That's something I don't want to do ever again."

She stood up. "It's time for you to go, Noah. Go back to your parents. I'll take care of the agents and the school."

That's not what he wanted to hear. After all Noah had been through, it was his fight just as much as anyone else's. He had friends back at the school, and he owed it to them to honor his word.

He grabbed her arm. "You can't! It's too dangerous to do this alone."

"You're sweet, and brave, but you don't understand how the dangerous it's going to get. I've dealt with them before. I'll be fine."

Noah crossed his arms. "But you don't know the school like I do. And there's the sentries. I also made a promise to my friends that I would help them, and I'm going to. With or without your help."

Ms. Vera stared at him, her gaze level without a trace of that warmth he was used to. "All right, Noah. You do know the school better than I do. But if at any point I think you're in too much danger, I'm getting you out of there."

Noah nodded, but he had no intention of leaving if things got dangerous.

My dad taught me to keep my promises.

CHAPTER 21

NOAH SQUIRMED in the back seat of Ms. Vera's small car, shimmying as best he could to make room and be somewhat comfortable. He was trapped between Jeff and Mika because he was the smallest one, like always. He buried his head into his chest as Ms. Vera glanced at him from the rearview mirror.

Ms. Vera wasn't happy. She didn't want to involve any more kids. But Noah had convinced her. They were going to break in anyway without her, so why not be with her?

"I can't believe we're doing this," Jeff said with a huge smile on his face. "Storming the school with our teacher no less! You didn't seem like the type, Ms. Vera."

"Don't get too excited about this, Jeff," Ms. Vera said. "If you kids are in danger, I'm getting you out of there right away."

"Yes, ma'am!" He leaned to Noah and whispered, "I'm pretty sure she's just talking about me and Mika."

"Thanks for letting us come along," Mika said, pushing her glasses up her nose. "I have some ideas on how we can get in."

"I'll bet," Ms. Vera said, glancing at the bags in the front seat, most of them Mika's. "Are you sure it's OK with your parents that you're out so late?" She adjusted the mirror to get a better look at them.

Mika nodded. "Uh-huh. My mom works late. As long as I left a note and call her, she won't mind."

"And you, Jeff?"

Jeff hesitated before looking away from her. "My dad doesn't care. You know how he is when it comes to parent-teacher conferences and things like that."

Mia sighed. "Unfortunately, I do. Once we get to the motel, I'll listen to your plan. If I like it and think it poses minimum risk to you three, we'll proceed with it, understood?"

The three kids looked at each other and rolled their eyes. Adults were always worried about the risks. It was no wonder they never got anything done. Even though Ms. Vera—Mia—could ghost, she was still an adult. The sooner they got to the motel, the sooner they could figure out what to do.

Noah sat in the passenger seat of the box delivery truck, glancing at the young white male to his left every few seconds. He knew it was his teacher that drove the truck, but it was going to take some getting used to. Calling his teacher Mia was one thing, but seeing her be someone else entirely was another.

"Noah," she said. "You're staring."

"Sorry," he said.

"That's OK. Remember the plan."

"How can we forget it?" Jeff said in Noah's earpiece.

"Yeah, this is way better than the walkie-talkies I brought," Mika said. "Thanks again for buying me all this stuff, Mia." Since Mika was new, she didn't have the same reservations Noah and Jeff had about calling her by her real name. "We have some high-quality tech here. With it, I'm sure we'll be able to breach the school."

Ms. Vera smiled. "Any time." But Noah couldn't help but wonder where she got all the money from.

The plan was for Ms. Vera and Noah to sneak into the school. The school may have been looking for Noah, but they wouldn't think that he'd return to the school. Even if they did, they didn't know that Ms. Vera was actually Mia. All they had to do was avoid the sentries. Ms. Vera could ghost into the other students or even Noah and sneak around until they found the control room. Once they did, they could shut down the devices in the students' necks and the sentries. Mika would handle anything technical, and Jeff would watch over Ms. Vera's body.

Noah looked toward the back of the delivery truck at Ms. Vera's body—the one he had known for years.

It was going to take some time getting used to her powers.

"You ready, Noah?" she said.

No, but Noah nodded. He had to at least try. He'd promised Elise and Jamal that he would.

"OK, quiet you guys," Ms. Vera said to his friends in the back. "Remember our plan. And if things get out of hand, surrender—and if I'm captured, tell them I forced you to come along."

"Yes, Ms. V," Jeff said. Jeff and Mika hid Mia's body between the boxes and other packages.

As they approached the gate to the back entrance of the school, Noah faded. He closed his eyes, remembering to breathe like his mother would have done in yoga, letting his power flow through him, making sure that he wasn't seen.

"Noah," Ms. Vera said, "your seatbelt."

Oh, right. Noah unbuckled his seatbelt and grasped the sides of his seat as the bumpy truck rode along.

The truck stopped at the gate. Noah looked through the truck's giant windows. He was afraid to see if a sentry was now at the gate. He let go of the edge of the seat, which he had grasped tightly. There wasn't one.

"Delivery for, uh..." Ms. Vera looked at the driver's device even though she didn't have to. "A Mrs. Crenshaw."

"Another one?" the guard said. "Jesus, that woman is always ordering packages here."

Ms. Vera shrugged. "Well, safer to have them delivered to work than home. Never know who might be stealing them."

"Ain't that right? See you around, Tom."

"Thanks."

Noah thought he could relax as they drove from the gates to the loading dock. That he'd get a moment's peace before they went through with their insane plan. But he couldn't. He was worried about the friends he had left behind. What had happened to them?

They arrived and Ms. Vera got out of the truck and brought Mrs. Crenshaw's package with her. Noah trailed her, staying back about ten feet, constantly looking out for the sentries or any of the agents with sunglasses. After all, they were the only ones who could see him.

Noah followed her, but then stopped when the driver's body hit the floor. He watched as another teacher—Mr. Shaw—came out of the restroom and dragged the driver's body back in. Mr. Shaw whispered, "blueberries."

Noah trailed her as she—Mr. Shaw—veered off and headed back to his classroom.

"Blueberries," a different teacher, Mrs. Chan, said from behind him as she walked by.

Noah had thought it would be easy shadowing her, but she switched bodies so fast and so often. He had to strain to hear her speak the code word.

The plan was to make it to the control room. They went from the loading docks, past the storage rooms, and ended up in the courtyard.

"Hey, how's it going you two?" Mika whispered into Noah's ear. "Sorry, but I can't access the school's files from here. I thought it'd be easy once I got into their server, but it's nothing like the movies."

"Is there anything I can do?" Jeff asked. "There doesn't seem to be anyone approaching the truck."

"Can the chatter, everyone," Ms. Vera said.

"Yes, Ms. V."

Noah still wasn't used to how cold and calculating Ms. Vera could be. She had always been so warm and caring, but these agents didn't bring that out in her. *I don't like that at all.*

Noah remembered the loving picture of her and her family. If they took away his family, he'd feel differently too. A part of him missed the teacher he once knew, but she was there now, helping him when she didn't have to.

Just like in class. He smiled.

Even though he had faded, Noah hated being exposed as they went. He darted from bush to bush, hiding as best as he could in the bright day light. Ms. Vera strolled with the package in hand, having stolen the body of Mrs. Crenshaw. She knew exactly where to go as Noah had told her and his friends the layout of the school. He'd even drawn a map for them.

Something's not right. Noah stopped. Everything was too quiet. They planned to sneak in when the students were on break. That way Ms. Vera could ghost into the students' bodies if necessary and there'd be the distraction of kids mulling about.

Ding. Ding. Ding.

Something's wrong. There should be no chime at this time unless it was for an assembly.

"I'm glad to see our newest student has returned to us," a familiar voice said over the intercom. "We were terribly worried about you."

Noah sucked in his breath and froze. This was a trap. There was no escape. He had been foolish to think he could rescue his friends from this school.

"Remember the plan," Ms. Vera said.

Noah nodded. They had already discussed what would happen if they got caught. The students were the most important thing to his teacher. She would help them escape.

"Noah," Mr. Cooper said, stepping out from one of the doors. With his dark shades on, Mr. Cooper looked directly at Noah. "I'm pleased to see you've come back." He looked at Ms. Vera. "Mrs. Crenshaw, don't be alarmed, but our friend Noah is right behind y ou."

"He is!" Ms. Vera said, nearly jumping. She peered around, astutely playing the part of a scared teacher. "My heavens. What is he doing here?"

Ms. Vera turned away from him and let out a small smile, nodding. There had been a possibility that one of them might get caught. If they did, one of them would continue on with the plan.

Noah glanced around, looking for ways to escape. When he glanced back the way they had come, a sentry appeared and another one came from behind Mr. Cooper. It was up to Ms. Vera now. He watched her slowly slither away.

"Noah," Mr. Cooper said, rubbing his temples. "I'm actually quite impressed that you managed to escape, especially with the safeguards we have in place now. You're the second fader to do so. It means you're far more advanced than we thought. And you've only scratched the surface of your powers."

Noah took a step back, never letting go of his power. There had to be something he could do. Some kind of ability that was part of his power that he was missing. He whispered into his earpiece, "Mika? Jeff? You there?"

Silence. Noah hoped they had gotten away, wherever they were.

"Seize him," Mr. Cooper said to the sentries. "But be gentle. Do not harm him."

"Understood."

The sentries stalked Noah, cutting him off from every angle of escape in the open courtyard. Ms. Vera and he should have split up, but Noah didn't want to be alone, making the mistake he'd seen in so many horror movies.

"Error," one of the sentries said. It turned its gaze toward Ms. Vera, who had only made it to the edge of the courtyard. "Singularity detected. Designation: ghost."

"Mrs. Crenshaw," Mr. Cooper said. "Or should I say ghost?" He pulled out a gun from his jacket. It was nothing Noah had seen before. It was sleek and shone with a silver sheen. "You're the one who incapacitated Elle. She wondered how you did it."

"I've come across you agents before," Ms. Vera said, clenching her fists and stepping back into the court-yard.

"You have, have you?" Mr. Cooper tapped his ear. "Then you know your abilities won't work against us. Sentries, carry out original orders, but also seize Mrs. Crenshaw. Use any means necessary."

"Affirmative," the sentries said.

"Noah, run!" Ms. Vera said.

Noah hesitated. This wasn't the plan. She should have left him when he got caught. Now she was going to go with the other plan of distracting them while Noah made his escape.

Noah hated to leave her, but he had to. He wouldn't waste her sacrifice. Noah ran, but one of the sentries moved to intercept him. He used his small frame and slid under the tall robot. But the robot's long reach grabbed him, yanking him by the back of his shirt.

Noah yelled. "Let me go!" He squirmed but his legs flailed several feet in the air.

No! He couldn't end here. He had made a promise to Elise and Jamal to get them out of here. He still wanted to see his parents. He just wanted to go home.

Noah reappeared and focused all his power. He released it into an aura around him, slamming it into the sentry.

The sentry released him, and Noah smiled. It had worked. He didn't know what he had done, but he realized he had a new ability to learn about.

"Noah, can you hear me?" Mika said in his ears.

"Yeah...what's up?" He smiled, relieved to hear his friends were OK.

"Me and Jeff found our way into the control room since you and Mia distracted the entire school. I was able to shut down the sentries."

"Oh, *you* shut down the sentries?"

"Yeah, why?"

Noah frowned, realizing that his power had done nothing to the advance robot. "Uh, no reason."

"Hey, I helped," Jeff said.

"Sure you did," Mika said. "I'm not sure how long the sentries will stay offline. In the meantime, I'm going to try to get as much information as I can from the school. They have loads of info on the students and their abilities."

"That's not the plan," Noah said. "I need to help my friends and the other students here."

"I know, but now is the perfect—"

A loud banging rang through Noah's ears.

"Uh, we gotta go," Jeff said. "We'll do what we can. If you don't hear from us, we'll meet you back at the truck. Catch ya later, buddy."

Noah smiled, thankful he had brought his friends along. Things hadn't gone exactly as planned, but they had found what they had been looking for and they'd managed to save him.

Ms. Vera had taken care of Mr. Cooper. She was now in another body, a slim teacher that Noah had seen around campus. As Noah ran to her, she picked up Mr. Cooper's gun.

"No!" Noah shouted. He didn't want her to kill Mr. Cooper, even if he was an agent.

Ms. Vera stared back at Noah with an icy glare. She lowered her gun and put it at the back of her waist.

She smiled at Noah but it lacked the warmth he was used to. "Come on, Noah. Let's go find the others and carry out the rest of the plan, OK?"

He nodded.

Without the sentries and the agents, it was easy to get around the school. There was no one to stop her. She zipped from body to body, thankfully, leaving them unharmed and unconscious.

They found the control room, the bored security guard Noah once saw now pounded on the thick door. "Get out here, you damn kids!" There was a keypad next to the door that the man turned his attention to. It was half opened and wires stuck out of it.

The man turned his attention to Noah, placing his hand on his weapon when he stopped, his body dropping to the floor.

Will I ever get used to that?

Ms. Vera opened the door and Noah said, "Hey guys, we're here." He looked around the small room but not seeing his friends anywhere.

Jeff peeked out from under the table. "Glad to see you. Whoa, who's that?"

Noah peeked over his shoulder, remembering that Ms. Vera was in a different body—a portly older teacher.

She smiled and said, "Blueberries. Where's Mika?"

"Here," she said, poking her head out of a vent in the ceiling. "We could have ran away but thought staying here would be better. Thank God you guys came." She squeezed and shimmied down into the room with her laptop. "That is going to take some getting used to." She stared at Ms. Vera.

"What have you learned?" their teacher asked.

Mika had a huge grin plastered on her face. "A lot! I downloaded some info from the servers. Have a ton more to sort through. But more importantly, I found out how they're shutting off the kids' powers with the chips in their necks."

Mika's hands danced on the control panel until she found a list of names with red lights next to them. "See here." She pointed and pushed up her glasses on her nose. "I can switch the light from red to green and give the kids back their powers."

"What are we waiting for?" Noah asked. "Do it."

"OK, but it's not that simple."

"What do you mean?" Ms. Vera asked.

"I *can* give them their powers but for how long? Someone else can reactivate the devices either here or remotely." She shrugged. "And they'll still have those devices in their necks."

"We can't worry about that now. They'll have to take care of that themselves. Turn all the devices off."

Mika grinned. "Sure thing."

All the lights beside the names turned green. Ms. Vera walked to the console and spoke into the microphone as Mika worked the controls. "Attention students. Thanks to your classmate—" She looked over at Noah and smiled. And despite being in a different body than he remembered, it was his teacher. "Noah Nobles, you are free to go. Class is dismissed."

Mika found the chime button and laughed. "It seemed appropriate."

"Perfect," Ms. Vera said. "Now stand back," She pulled out her gun, aiming it at the console before firing.

"Wait!" Mika said, stretching out her hand, but Noah held her back.

"We need to go. Meet me back at the truck while I switch bodies."

Mika stared at the destroyed console and shook her head. "I really wish she hadn't done that. I barely scratched the surface of this school. There was more to learn."

"You downloaded enough files," Jeff said. "This isn't the library. I wanna get outta here. All this sneaking around has made me hungry."

Noah ran after his friends, and throughout the school, students peeked their heads out. One door turned into flowers and fell to the ground. Kids rushed out of the classrooms, some using their powers, and others not. Teachers yelled for them to come back. Noah had to dodge the students as if they were trees.

One student grabbed his arm. "Noah! You did it!" Elise bent down and squeezed Noah into a hug before giving him a kiss on the cheek. He blushed.

"Who's this?" Mika asked, crossing her arms.

"My friend," Noah said. "I told you about her."

"Don't worry," Elise said. "We're just friends. He's not my type."

Mika scowled at her.

"I can't believe you actually did it," Elise said. "I didn't think you'd be able to do it. I was glad that you could get away. I didn't think you'd come back here even if Jamal did."

"Yeah, well, I had help." Noah looked over his shoulder at his friends.

"Thanks," Elise said and smiled.

"It's not over," Mika said, pushing up her glasses. "You still need to remove the tracker in your neck."

"I will, but first I need to get out of here. Can we go? I assume however you snuck in here is the way you're leaving."

"Yeah," Noah said. "But what about Jamal?"

She rolled her eyes. "He'll be fine."

"No, we should get him. If it wasn't for him, I wouldn't have found out about you. None of this would have happened!"

Elise grabbed him by the shoulders. "I know, Noah. But we don't have time for this. You're going to have to trust me. Jamal can take care of himself."

Noah bit his lip and looked down. He didn't want to leave Jamal behind but she was right. He was old enough to look out for himself. That's the one thing Noah knew about Jamal, even if he didn't know what powers he had.

"OK."

Jeff and Mika led them out of the school, and Noah struggled to keep up with his taller friends. Along the way, Elise gathered as many of the confused students as she could, corralling them and yelling at them, "Come with us!" But there was one person she missed amidst the chaos.

Riley.

Riley stood in the courtyard, watching students run, fly, and even hop away.

Noah broke away from the others and ran to Riley. He grabbed his arm. "Come on. We need to go!"

Riley yanked his arm away, tears running down his face. "What did you do? You ruined everything!"

Noah pulled away. "What do you mean? I set you all free."

"No, you didn't! I warned you. Some of us enjoyed being here. The school helped us learn more about our powers, and we weren't a danger to those we cared about."

Riley put his hands to his head and shut his eyes. Noah crept forward and said, "Hey Riley. Remember the games. Remember how you're able to control your powers now."

"No! You're wrong! And this is why I told the school about how you were gonna come back and rescue everyone!"

Noah stepped back. He couldn't believe that his friend had betrayed him to the agents. After all Noah had done for him. He had helped him control his powers and played board games with him. *How could he? Fine.* If that was the case, then Noah would leave him at the mercy of the school.

Noah turned to leave but stopped. He turned around. Riley closed his eyes, sitting on the ground, rocking himself back and forth. It reminded Noah of when they first met.

I can't leave him here. He needs help. We all do.

Noah walked over and held his hand out. "Come on."

"What are you doing?"

Noah smiled. "Getting my friend out of here so he can see his family."

Riley took his hand.

"You ready?"

"Thanks, but I already told you I'm not going any-where. I like it here. And with less kids, maybe it won't be so loud in my mind."

Noah opened his mouth but shut it and nodded. "Maybe you can teach me another game next time I see you."

Riley smiled. "Yeah, I'd like that."

Noah left his friend and ran back to the delivery truck.

By the time Noah got back to the truck, nearly two dozen kids were crammed into it. Ms. Vera had returned to the driver's body.

"There you are," Elise said. "We were worried about you. What took you so long?"

"I had to see Riley."

Elise reached out and squeezed his hand. "Understood." She pointed to the front. "We left the front seat of the vehicle for you."

"I don't know. Maybe another, bigger kid should sit up there. I'm fine being squeezed back here."

"Nonsense. You belong here. If it wasn't for you, we wouldn't have made it away from the school."

All the kids stared at him and Noah scratched his arm, wanting to fade.

Elise led Noah to the front of the vehicle. As Noah walked by, they smiled and patted him on the back.

Ms. Vera, still in the driver's body, grinned and winked at Noah. "OK, kids. Hang on, don't step on my body, and we'll be out of here in no time."

The kids roared in delight.

Ms. Vera had driven them toward the edge of the city where the homeless camps encroached upon the tech companies downtown.

"Are you sure you want me to drop you all off here?" Ms. Vera asked.

"Yeah," Elise said, helping the other kids off the truck. "Wouldn't be the first time some of us have been in areas like this." She shrugged. "There's a lot of other kids not from around here. Gotta figure out how to get them home."

"I have more money I can give you if you go back with us," Ms. Vera said.

Elise shook her head. "No time." She scratched the back of her neck. "We still need to get these out of us. The school did teach us a lot about our powers." She grinned. "With our new abilities, we'll be fine. Trust me."

One by one, Elise hugged Jeff, Mika, and Ms. Vera. "Thanks again for helping us." She hugged Noah and squeezed him tighter than the others, whispering into his ear. "And thank you. You're a good person, Noah. You're far braver than your size. Don't ever forget that." She pulled back and smiled, tears hovering in her eyes.

"Are you going to be OK?" Noah asked. "Like really?" He glanced at her long sleeves, worried about what he'd find beneath.

She sniffled tears away. "I think I am. Thanks to you. I guess Jamal was right about you...for once."

"Where do you think he is?"

She grimaced. "Causing trouble, no doubt."

"I didn't get a chance to say goodbye to him."

Elise rubbed Noah's afro. "It's for the best. He's a difficult teenager, but he did believe in you. As did we all. So he was right about something...for once."

Elise kissed him on the forehead.

As the stream of kids and teenagers walked by Noah, Troi stopped in front of him and offered him a piece of gum. She grinned. "I liked this plan much better."

She caught up to the others and they disappeared into the city.

"Can we get something to eat?" Jeff asked. "Being a hero has made me hungry."

Despite Ms. Vera's objections, they ended up in a diner. Ms. Vera kept a constant lookout, ghosting into each new person that walked in, Jeff ate his weight in food, and Mika barely touched a bite at all, absorbed by all the information she had downloaded from the school. Noah ate most of his food, but he was content to be with his friends and teacher.

It's over. It's finally over.

Mika made a squeaking noise. "I can't believe it."

"OK," Jeff said. "Are you finally going to tell us what you've been reading all this time? You've barely said a word to us."

"I don't know. Are you finally going to stop eating?"

Jeff made a face and quickly snatched the last fries on Noah's plate.

Mika pushed up her glasses. "There's all sorts of info on the students. They were...I don't know how to say this? Studying them."

Noah sat up in the booth. "How so?"

"They were testing you. They were learning about you and your abilities as much as you were. Not just in gym, but some of the students, mostly older ones, were in special classes where they could use their powers." Mika stared at the computer as she dug through some more information. "Did you know there was a girl who had chameleon-like powers? At first, they only worked when she didn't move. Very weird. And there was a boy who could literally blow smoke. As for you..."

"What about me?"

"Ummm...this is a theory. Don't know if it's true, but it's what they think may happen."

Noah, Ms. Vera, and Jeff stared at her, but she didn't say anything. She continued to stare at the screen, her eyes getting wider.

"What is it?" Noah asked, steadying his hand.

"I don't know if I should tell you. You're not going to like it."

"Go ahead and tell him," Ms. Vera said. "You yourself said it was only a theory."

Mika shrugged. "Well, it is but it's also backed up by the evidence they gathered."

"Please," Noah said. "Just tell me. I need to know."

"OK, don't say I didn't warn you." Mika leaned forward into the screen. "They say you have the power to fade from people's minds and machines. That's how your power works. You don't disappear like the invisible man. Based on that, they believe you can make anyone forget you permanently." Mika looked up from her screen and stared directly at him. "And that you were close to achieving it."

"That's cool," Jeff said. "He has a new power."

"Uh-uh. That's not all." She traced her finger along the screen. "It says here that there's also a chance that he may completely fade from the world. You'll be forgotten and no longer part of the world."

Noah froze, unable to move or speak. While he loved his powers and had accepted them as part of himself, he couldn't imagine not existing. What would his friends and teacher think? And what about his parents? *They'd forget about me.*

Ms. Vera grabbed his hand. He finally breathed again and reached out to finish the almost-full glass of water in front of him.

"Will it say how?" his teacher asked. "If he uses too much of his power or...mindwipes people, will that be how he fades forever?"

Mika shook her head. "Some of them think so. One thinks it's just the...natural progression of his powers. The problem is they've only had two in hand. One being the one kid who escaped before Noah and the other being Noah. They knew of two more in the last few decades, but could never catch them."

Noah slumped back in the booth.

"Don't look so glum," Jeff said. "It's not fact. It's only a theory."

Noah lifted his head and gave his friend a tired smile. He didn't believe it. "I hope you're right."

"Sure I am. Can we order some pie? It'll make you feel better."

Noah didn't eat much pie, but Jeff ate it all. As Ms. Vera drove them back, Noah couldn't help but think of Mika's words. *Will I disappear?* He stared at his hands and imagined his body slowly fading from the world like grains of sand slipping through your fingers. He had to tell his parents. They needed to know. But he couldn't do it alone.

While Ms. Vera and Jeff didn't agree with Noah's decision, they supported him in doing so. All three of them were going to go with Noah to tell his parents about his abilities and the school they had sent him to.

They arrived at Noah's house and a big grin formed on his face. He unbuckled his seat belt and leapt from the car, not waiting for it to come to a complete stop. He was anxious to run into his house to hug his parents and be swept into their arms. He ignored the pleas of his friends and teacher. He got to the front door, digging in his pockets for his keys, but remembered that he didn't have them.

"Hey, wait for us!" Jeff said.

Noah rang the doorbell and waited. As much as he ached to see his parents, he was glad his friends and teacher were there. His parents would be far more forgiving with Ms. Vera there. She would help back up what Noah had been through. For some reason, adults only ever believed other adults, even though they lied a lot. Noah had ditched school, after all and the agents would have told his parents a lie.

The door opened. Noah's smile faded and he backed away.

"Mr. Cooper," he said.

CHAPTER 22

NOAH TURNED to Ms. Vera, but she didn't budge. She didn't even say a word. When Noah saw Ms. Luna behind Mr. Cooper, that's when he realized why.

Noah, Mika, and Jeff backed away from the door. Mr. Cooper didn't have his sunglasses on, and Noah knew he could fade and leave him. But he couldn't leave his friends behind.

"What's wrong with Ms. V?" Jeff asked. "Why ain't she moving?"

"It's the timestopper," Mika said. "She's keeping her in place. The good news is that to completely stop one person without slowing down the surrounding area, she has to fully focus on that person."

"Insightful," Mr. Cooper said. He stepped onto the porch past Ms. Vera. "And you must be Noah's friend Mikayla. You're very bright. I also take it you're the one who broke into our files."

Mika glared at him. "So what if I did?"

"What did you do to my parents?" Noah asked.

"Nothing. I'm not a monster, despite what some students may think. Please, I implore you to come with me to the school and learn more about your powers. There's still more you don't know about yourself."

Noah stared at his hands. *I do need to learn more about my powers.* He shook his head. He would learn more about himself—not in the school, but with his friends and family.

Jeff leaned into Noah and whispered, "Run, he can't see you without his glasses. I'll cover for you like I did that one time with Francis."

Noah couldn't help but smile at the memories. As much as he didn't want to run, they needed help.

"Guys," Mika said. "We have company."

"I'm disappointed in you, Noah," Mr. Cooper said. "You leave me no choice."

Three sentries came from behind Mr. Cooper. They fanned out, encroaching on and encircling the kids.

"Be careful," Noah said. "It's the sentries I told you about." But all of their eyes were focused on Noah. He was the one with the powers.

Jeff picked up a small rock and threw it at the sentry. It bounced off its skin like hide.

Noah stared at him and shook his head.

Jeff shrugged. "It was worth a shot."

"You have no idea how dangerous these robots are," Mika said. "If you did, you wouldn't provoke them."

"Do you know of a weakness?" Jeff asked. "Can you shut them down or turn them off?"

She tilted her head. "If I had a computer, ten minutes, a good Wi-Fi signal, and peace and quiet, then maybe I might get one of them to stop. Maybe."

"If I go with him," Noah said. "Maybe he'll leave you guys alone."

Mika shook her head. "No. We're in this together. Um...but I'm not sure what we can do. We're just kids."

"You know, I had a hard time finding this place," said a familiar voice from the sidewalk. "This is a nice neighborhood though." He whistled. "Sure wish I lived here growing up."

"Jamal!" Noah said.

Jamal tilted his head. "How's it going, mushroom?"

Jeff snorted with laughter. "Is that what they call you? I see it."

"Shut up."

"Jamal," Mr. Cooper asked. "What are you doing here?"

Jamal strolled closer with his hands in his pockets but stopped before his feet touched the grass. "Nice lawn. Always wished I had one." He bent down to the grass, ripped out a handful, and inhaled it through his nose. "Ahhh." He let the blades of grass fall from his fingers.

"I apologize, mushroom. I was rude. I came because I didn't say goodbye before I left. You held up your end of the bargain, but I didn't hold up mine."

"Does he always talk this much?" Mika asked.

"Sometimes," Noah said. "Elise hates it."

"Maybe he's buying us time," Jeff said, shrugging.

Jamal waved his finger. "But I wasn't the only one who wanted to say goodbye."

Jamal's shadow stretched until it left him. *Inky,* Noah remembered. Noah followed Jamal's gaze to the roof of his home. The duo slapped their hands together, lighting up the night sky, forming one person. More and more of the School of Expressive and Extraordinary Young People's students surrounded Jamal—nearly three dozen kids.

"Sentries, subdue and detain the students," Mr. Cooper said, putting his sunglasses on. "Elle, help with the confinement." He pulled out his silver gun.

"Attack!" Jamal yelled.

One of the older students, picked up a handful of dirt and blew it at one of the sentries. The dirt blossomed into a hand and clung to the machine. She grinned, squeezing her hand and tightening her grip on the sentry.

The dirt around the sentry exploded. The sentry's inhuman eyes glowed red and it stomped toward the girl. Everything she threw at it—dirt, grass, dandelions—had no effect on it. She scrambled backward to escape it when her foot slipped. The sentry reached out to her, and a large round ball smashed into it, crashing the sentry into a tree.

The ball unfurled into another kid. Ball Boy smiled before helping her up.

Mr. Cooper lifted his weapon and fired his gun. Instead of a bullet, a circular beam of light shot out from it, encompassing a student. She flailed her arms and screamed before hitting the dirt.

The ground beneath Noah rumbled. A huge bump rippled on top of the dirt, heading straight for Mr. Cooper. Before it could reach the teacher, one of the sentries dove its arm into the ground. When it pulled its arm out, a young girl struggled against the sentry's strong grip until she went unconscious.

Ball Boy bounced his way around, smashing into that sentry and ricocheting off the ground and off a nearby tree. He built up momentum, bouncing toward Mr. Cooper. Mr. Cooper didn't waver as the boy flew to him. The agent leveled his gun and fired it at Ball Boy. Ball Boy unfurled from his rolled-up state and smacked into the porch. He shook like he had a seizure.

"The gun," Mika said. "It doesn't fire real bullets at you. It has multiple settings. Right now, it's been set to interrupt your powers for a short time. Painful from what I read."

"Jesus, he never misses," Jeff said. "Even my dad would be impressed. Not very fast though."

"Look at how the tip of the gun dims after it fires. It requires a three-second charge. And the glasses help him aim." Mika hummed in thought. "Those glasses are some kind of super computer. It does more than we can see. I gotta get my hands on a pair."

The students had taken down one sentry, but between the other two and the agents, the battle was turning against the kids.

"Hey, buddy," Jeff said, "remember that one time you and I took out Francis?"

A wide smile crossed Noah's face. Of course. It was the *only* time they got the drop on Francis.

Noah faded and ran toward Mr. Cooper, hoping that fighting with the older kids took the agent's attention away and that he wouldn't see him. The plan was to bowl into Mr. Cooper's long legs, getting him to drop the gun.

Noah was six feet away from him, picking up steam, when Mr. Cooper turned his focus away from the ensuing fray to point his gun directly at him. Mr. Cooper sighed. "Noah, I'm disappointed in you."

A blast shot out from the gun. Noah yelled as it disrupted his powers and he crashed to the ground. His body froze up and it was like a million bees stung him all at once. When Noah came to, Mr. Cooper towered over him with a pair of restraints in his hand.

"The first lesson is always the hardest," Mr. Cooper said.

Right when he was about to clamp down the restraints on Noah, Jeff roared, "Yeehaw!" And the gangly young kid smashed into the agent from the side and Mr. Cooper sprawled into the ground.

Noah crawled over to check on his friend. "Yee-haw?"

Jeff rolled until he sat upright. "It was all I could think of." He rubbed his shoulder. "He's a lot sturdier than he looks."

The friends shared a laugh.

Mr. Cooper got up. His sunglasses had fallen away and so had his gun, but that was still within reach. The deceptively friendly face darkened with anger. He grabbed the gun, adjusted the setting and aimed it at Noah. "This is going to hurt but it's for your own good."

Noah closed his eyes, the sweat dripping down his forehead. He opened his eyes to see Mr. Cooper smiling at him.

"Blueberries," he said.

"Ms. Vera!" Noah said. He covered his hands with his mouth, hoping no one had heard him in the fray.

Ms. Vera left Noah and said to the two remaining sentries. "Stand down. I order you to return to base."

"What in the world are you doing, Charles?" Ms. Luna asked.

Ms. Vera pointed the gun and shot Ms. Luna. It stunned Ms. Luna into unconsciousness, her scream was far worse than Noah's. Mr. Cooper's body dropped to the ground as Ms. Vera returned to her own body on the lawn.

The sentries stalked back toward the school. The students powered down and helped those who had been bound, shot, or injured.

Jamal strolled over to Noah. "Always knew you had it in you," Jamal said, grinning. "The others thought you were too small. Me, I knew better."

"What made you come to my house, and how'd you get all these other kids to help?" Noah asked.

Jamal smirked. "I told you to say goodbye, and it was quite a show. Worth coming all the way out here."

Noah wasn't falling for Jamal's false bravado. Not after tonight. "No, really."

Jamal bent down until he was the same height as Noah. "Adults, they're not to be trusted even if they are one of us." He glanced at Ms. Vera but she didn't say a word. "Those at the school are worse. They're dangerous, and so are you. I knew they'd be back for you, and I knew they'd come to your parents' place. You have a loving family, mushroom. A lot of us always wished we could have it. But it's also your weakness. They'll exploit it."

Jamal walked away but Noah ran up and grabbed his arm.

"Yes, mushroom? Didn't think you'd miss me so much." He winked. "I promise not to tell Elise."

Noah smiled, shaking his head. "That's not it. Before you go, you owe me."

"Oh. After what I just did, *I* owe *you?*" Jamal laughed. "That's a good one."

"You never told me what you can do, and I didn't see it tonight. I want to know."

Jamal was quiet, cupping his hand to his chin. He bent down and whispered, "Stand on your head."

"Wha—" An itching sensation crept up Noah's arms. One so strong, it couldn't be scratched with his fingers. Next thing he knew, he found himself standing on his head.

Jamal chuckled and waved as he walked away. "You make a hell of a misfit, mushroom. Maybe I'll see you around."

As the kids left, each thanking Noah in their own way, he couldn't help but wonder if Jamal had forced the other kids to come.

But he couldn't think of that now. There was only one thought on his mind—his parents.

Noah sprinted inside the house yelling, "Mom! Dad!"

His heart dropped when he found his parents unconscious on the living room couch. His mood lightened when they snored. They were alive and fine! Noah gently woke them up.

"Noah?" Dad asked, yawning. "What are you doing here?"

"Shoes," Mom said, making a face and rubbing her eyes. "Take off your shoes."

But Noah disobeyed her. "Mom, Dad. Are you all right?"

"Of course we're all right," Dad said. "We were talking with Mr. Cooper and his assistant when…" He looked at Mom. "What exactly did happen, dear? I remember talking with them and then I found our son here."

Mom reached out to Noah and took his hands. "What are you doing here? At this time. What's going on?"

Noah saw their confused and concerned faces. He exhaled and nodded. It was time to tell them the truth. "OK, I'll tell you."

"But first," Mom said, glaring at him. "Take off your shoes."

Noah grinned. "Yes, Mom."

After they had tied and secured the agents, Ms. Vera, Jeff, and Mika joined Noah and his family in the living room. They let Noah tell his side of the story. He told his parents everything, but only after he and the others took off their shoes. He was worried how his parents would react. While they asked questions, they didn't seem mad. Of course he wasn't sure if they fully believed him either. Which was why when Noah was done with his story, he had to show them.

"Where did you go?" Mom asked. "One second you were in front of me and then the next you were gone."

"Poof!" Dad said, "like a magic trick we saw in Vegas that one time."

"That's right, Dad."

"It's far more than that," Ms. Vera said, sitting with her arms crossed. "Mr. and Mrs. Noble, your son has powers only a selective few have."

"And Ms....Mia," Mom said. "You also have this power?"

"Yes, but mine is different."

"And those agents he spoke of will never leave him alone?"

Ms. Vera shook her head. "In my experience, no. I once had a family like you, but they took it away from me."

"I'm sorry."

"Then what do we do?" Noah asked. "I can't return to the school and I can't stay here."

"He's right," Dad said. He stood up. "Let's go get you packed. We'll hide out at my sister's for a day or two while we plan our next move. We have enough money to last for a few months if we stretch it."

"Then what happens?" Noah asked. "We can't keep running away. They'll keep hunting us and won't leave us alone, just like they did with Ms. Vera!"

Noah's parents looked to their son's teacher, but she didn't say anything.

"Let's get packing and we can talk about this later," Dad said.

Sometimes adults could be just as shortsighted as kids. Noah knew they didn't know what they would do after that. He didn't want to uproot and ruin his family's lives. He knew his parents would do anything for him because they loved him. But he was the one with the powers and the responsibility. Not them. And he had to do something helpful with his powers.

"Hey, Jeff and Mika, can you wait outside with Ms. Vera? I'll be with you in a few minutes. We're just gonna pack and I'll be right out."

"Are you sure?" Mika asked.

"Yeah. Trust me."

Ms. Vera said, "I'll be in the car waiting." But the way she looked at Noah, it was as if she knew what he was going to do.

"Why'd you have them wait?" Mom said. "We have our own car. Wherever we're going, we can meet them there. Besides, Mia has to drop the kids off, and we need to make it to your Aunt Lydia's before it's too late."

Noah bit his lip. "Can you help me pack? I don't know what's important, and I have so much stuff."

"Sure thing," Dad said. "It'll be like camping. Remember that?"

Noah smiled but it was a sad one. "Yeah, Dad. I remember."

They went to Noah's room and his parents packed his suitcase. They were always good at packing the necessities. Noah grabbed his backpack, dumping out all the schoolwork. He packed his backpack, this time only taking what he thought was necessary to him. That included all his art supplies and blank notebooks. There was one more important thing to him.

Noah reached under his bed and pulled out a small box. He opened it up, glimpsing dozens of pictures taken over the years. Most of them were of his family while they were out on vacation or going to the zoo or a haunted house. There were a few with his cousins and some of him and Jeff.

Noah had thought that having physical pictures was a waste. That it took up space. You could have more pictures, accessible anywhere, and it could all fit in your hand. But his parents were from a different generation. While he didn't understand all the things his parents did, this was one he was thankful for, and he now knew why some people didn't store things digitally.

Noah stuffed the box in his backpack and followed his parents downstairs.

"Emma, now that we've done all the work for Noah." Dad winked at his son. "We've got our own packing to do."

"I don't even know where to begin. I have so much stuff."

"And so many clothes and shoes."

Mom glared at Dad. He smiled and slunk away.

"Wait!" Noah said. "You don't need to pack any-thing."

Mom cocked her head. "We don't?"

"No. You guys aren't going anywhere. It's too dan-gerous for you."

Mom rubbed Noah's shoulder. "I know it'll be tough, but it'll be OK. We'll be here for you. Have faith."

"Yeah, son," Dad said, coming closer. "We'll get through this together like we always have."

Noah wrapped his arms around his parents and squeezed, building up his power. "I love you."

"We love you too."

"And I'm gonna miss you. You can't go with me."

"Son," Mom said, "What are—"

Noah released his built-up power, slamming it into both of his parents. Their eyes rolled to the backs of their heads and they fell backward. Noah collapsed on top of his parents. His chest heaved with each breath and his eyes were heavy. It was a weird feeling using his power like that. But he knew that all the memories his parents had of him were gone. It was safer that way for their sake.

Noah held tightly onto them. He kissed them on their foreheads, sniffling away the tears falling down his cheeks.

It wasn't an easy decision but Noah couldn't let his parents uproot their lives and force them into harm's way. Ms. Vera...no, Mia...was right. The agency wouldn't stop. He wasn't going to make the same mistakes his teacher had made. He couldn't live with himself if anything happened to his parents.

Noah rushed to the door, taking one more photograph with him. It was of last Halloween, and they were each dressed like a vampire. His dad was the Count from Sesame Street, his mom was Dracula, and he was the one that sparkled.

He took one last look around the only home he had ever known. He smiled at the memories he had of his ten years of life and at his parents. "I love you, Mom, Dad."

CHAPTER 23

BY THE TIME Noah got to the car, he'd done his best to wipe away his tears and running nose at making the most difficult decision of his young life.

"Hey, what took you so long?" Jeff asked. "Some of us have gotta go home and eat dinner."

"Is food always on your mind?" Mika asked.

Noah slid into the back seat with all his belongings. Mika was also back there with him. Jeff sat up front.

"What about your parents?" Jeff asked. "They coming?"

"They'll...they'll meet us there after we drop you off.

"OK." Jeff settled back into his seat.

Mika stared at Noah. He buckled at her gaze, turning and wiping another tear away.

She leaned over and in a quiet voice asked, "Is everything all right?"

"It's fine." His voice croaked. He wasn't fine. It was more than just erasing his parents' memories. Using that much power, all at once, took a lot out of him.

"Are you sure? You can talk to me." She reached out and grabbed his hand.

"I know." Noah gently squeezed her hand before snatching it away.

Noah's eyes met Ms. Vera's eyes in the rearview mirror. But she didn't say a word.

Noah walked Jeff to his front door. Jeff kept his voice low. "You didn't have to walk me to my door. I don't want you to run into my dad. You know how he is."

"I know. I just wanted to thank you for your help. You didn't have to come."

Jeff's eyes widened. "Are you kidding me? This is the most fun I've had in years. You know I'm always gonna help you whenever you need something."

"I know. I'm going to miss you."

Jeff squirmed. "Don't be like that. You're gonna keep in touch, right? Send me some drawings. Call me from time to time."

Noah put his fingertips to Jeff's forehead.

"What are you doing?"

"Goodbye, Jeff. Thanks for being my best friend."

Noah shot his power into Jeff, this time focusing it into Jeff's mind instead of scattering it all over like he did with his parents. It was easier to do that a second time, and he didn't feel quite as winded. Noah caught Jeff when he fell over and gently set him in front of the door. He rang the doorbell then ran back to the car.

"What happened?" Mika asked when Noah got in the car.

"I didn't want to see his dad. You don't know how he is."

"So very true," Ms. Vera said.

Ms. Vera drove Mika home and not much was said. However, Mika kept glancing at him out of the corner of her eye and Noah sighed. He couldn't take much more of it.

"We're here," his teacher said.

"Thanks, Mia," Mika said. "I wish I got to know you as a teacher. I'm sure you were a good one."

"She's the best," Noah said.

Ms. Vera smiled. "Thank you, Noah. I would have loved to have had you in my class. You're very bright, Mika. Never let them take that from you."

She grinned. "I'll try."

"Good."

Noah walked Mika to the door in silence. He was going to have to erase her memory of him. Would it be easier since they had only known each other for a short time? But she had helped him when she didn't have to. She was a friend just like Jeff was. He wished they had gotten to know each other more.

"You're quiet," Mika said.

"Sorry, been a long day, and using my powers this much has exhausted me."

"I bet. Mindwiping people can do that. Thinking about mindwiping me too?"

Noah stopped on the apartment complex's sidewalk. "Wh-what? No. I...I wouldn't."

Mika peered over her large glasses, angry eyes staring at him. "Noah. Don't play me for a fool."

He opened his mouth then shut it. "You're right. Sorry."

"What I don't understand is why."

"Because I don't wanna put you guys in any more danger."

Mika pushed her glasses up and she pointed a finger at him. "You don't get to decide that, Noah. We helped you out with the school and at your house. We were even there for you in the beginning."

"Yeah, but—"

"But what?"

Tears hovered in Noah's eyes. "I was worried about you, Mika! Miss Vera can handle herself, but I had to worry about you, Jeff, my parents, Elise, Jamal, Riley, and all the other students. I promised them I would free them, and I was afraid of what would happen to you. You don't know what it's like! That much responsibility!"

He crouched on the ground, letting the tears fall from his eyes, no longer caring if Mika saw it. His sobs grew louder while his voice shrank quieter. "And now my parents and my best friend won't remember me at all. And what's worse is that I'll never forget them."

Mika knelt down, cupping Noah's chin, forcing him to meet her eyes. "Oh Noah, you don't have to go through this alone. You don't have to make us forget you."

He sniffled. "I wish you were right."

"It's your choice. You don't have to. I'll never forget you."

Before Noah could answer, Mika leaned over and kissed him. It was Noah's first kiss. He had no idea what he was doing, but he kissed her back with all the feelings he had for her.

Noah used that moment to mindwipe Mika. He caught her as she fell back, unconscious. He knew that if she spoke, she would be the one person to talk him out of it. He put her bag underneath her head and said, "I'm sorry, Mika. Ms. Vera is right. They'll never stop and I don't want any harm to come to you either. You mean a lot to me." He gently kissed her forehead. "You won't remember me, but I'll never forget you."

Noah knocked on her apartment door. This time, Mika's mom was there. He said she needed his help as Mika had passed out on the way back. Noah brought her to her daughter and faded away.

Noah returned to the car and to his teacher. He needed her help. She was the only one who understood. But what if she didn't want to help him? What if she didn't understand what he did?

"Ms. Vera, I..." He took a deep breath. "Can I stay with you?"

She turned in her car seat and said, "What happened?"

Noah told her how he'd used his powers to mind-wipe those he cared about. And how it was the hardest thing he had ever done.

When he was finished, Ms. Vera wrapped Noah in her arms. He cried his eyes out, wishing that his mother were there to comfort him instead of his favorite teacher.

Ms. Vera soothed him. "Shhh. It'll be OK, Noah. Of course you can stay with me." She wiped away his tears with her hands and gave him a warm smile. "You've made a hard decision. Far harder than any decisions I've had to make, especially at your age.

"You can stay with me, Noah, and I will care for you as long as you like, but I don't plan on running away from the agency, or hiding from them. Not after I've found out what they do to you kids. Not anymore. It's time to take the fight to them."

Noah pulled away from his teacher and wiped his eyes. "What do you mean?"

CHAPTER 24

CHARLES COOPER stood in front of the Nobles' residence with the morning sun beginning its daily journey. He prodded the bandage around his head, nursing a terrible headache. The cleanup crew was busy retrieving the pieces of the sentry. And there was still the matter of the neighbors he would have to deal with.

"You all right?" Elle asked, walking up to him.

"Christ, no. I won't be all right. How could we screw up like this?" He ran his fingers through his thick hair. "So many singularities gone."

"You underestimated Noah."

Charles shook his head. "Uh-uh. He had help. That ghost of his. Noah could have been a great asset of ours. I could feel it."

Elle snorted.

"What about the parents? How are they taking it?"

Elle glanced back at the house. "'Bout as well as you'd expect. They remember you and me, but not a son. And it doesn't help that their house is covered in pictures of the three of them, not to mention their phones and computers."

"Total erasure," Charles said. "That's an advanced technique. Didn't think he had it in him. I wonder if he knows what it cost him?" He was silent, thinking about all the abilities Noah had and how they could backfire. That's why he and other kids like him needed their help.

"What about the friends?" Charles asked. "They helped—Christ. As if things couldn't get worse."

A nondescript black car drove up to the residence. An older woman stepped out. She surveyed the scene around, her hard and weathered face showing little emotion before barking orders at those around her. Those hard eyes stared at Charles and she stalked closer to him.

"Zelda," Charles said under his breath. "Here she comes."

"Quite a mess you've made, Charles," she said.

"I'm cleaning it up." He made it a point to meet her gaze. He had to show her that he wasn't afraid of her. Although he knew with her background and history, he should be. "We have almost total containment."

Zelda's eyebrows rose. "'Total containment?' Is that what you call it? I didn't realize a breach of the school, hundreds of students escaping, property damage, and one destroyed sentry was considered 'containment.'"

"Ma'am," Elle said, "We captured almost half of the students. Estimates have us getting up to eighty percent by the end of the week. And new security measures have been put in place for the school. We—"

"See to it then," Zelda said.

Elle looked to Charles before walking away.

"I wish you wouldn't do that," Charles said. "She's a good assistant. She shows that the program works, and she's helped track down a lot of the students."

"And I wish you didn't create this mess." Zelda reached into her coat pocket, but her hand came out empty. "I also wish I still smoked. We can't all get what we want. What about the boy's friends?"

"I've already sent a team there. I was just about to head there myself, but I doubt we'll get anything. If Noah erased his parents' minds, then—"

"Then he might have done the same to his friends." Zelda sighed. "Go there, and I'll see to things here."

"Yes, ma'am." Charles started to walk away, thankful to get away.

"You were lucky. The ghost could have killed you and Elle. I'm surprised she didn't. Must have been the kid's influence."

"You know her?"

Zelda nodded. "Oh yes. Her name is Amelia. Goes by Mia."

Charles slapped his forehead. "Christ. I didn't realize it was her. I've read the reports."

"I've been there. She's caused so much destruction throughout the agency, and twice I've almost had her." Zelda gave a tight-lipped smile and it chilled Charles. "It's been years since our last encounter. I never imagined she would be a schoolteacher. She must have taken to it just like her husband. Amir was a good man. I'm sorry about what happened to him." Her voice was heavy—heavier than he had ever heard it.

Zelda put on the same sunglasses Charles wore and her face hardened. "Clean up your mess and report back to me."

"Yes, ma'am." Charles paused. A question popped in his mind as he remembered the face of the school teacher. "Do you think we'll see Mia again?"

"Now that we've ruined her peaceful life for the third time?" Zelda raised her eyebrows. "I have no doubt."

Author's Corner

Email: marcjohnson@marcanthonyjohnson.com

Facebook: http://www.facebook.com/MarcJohnsonAuthor

Goodreads: http://www.goodreads.com/marcjohnson

Newsletter: https://rb.gy/6ru8lc

Twitter: http://www.twitter.com/Hellsfire

Website: http://www.marcanthonyjohnson.com

www.ingramcontent.com/pod-product-compliance
Lightning Source LLC
Chambersburg PA
CBHW031307210726
48287CB00005B/1455